The Brackman Ticket

Paperback Edition

N.L. Mayers

Gerrie House Publishing

Paperback Edition

Scripture quotations are taken from the King James version of the Bible; public domain of the United States of America

The Navy Hymn; public domain of the United States of America

ISBN: 979-8-9999280-1-6

DEDICATION

This book is dedicated to the Man who bought the ticket

Chapter One

Honolulu, Hawaii, January 1943

Brian Jackson—Jack to nearly everyone—hated how the ocean gave a guy the illusion of relief. Spray from the vessel's wake sparkled in the sun. The Pacific stretched endlessly, cool and inviting. But inside the ship, the temperature at dawn read ninety-five degrees.

Like all carriers in the Pacific, the *USS New Yorker* was hot. Water droplets condensed on pipes, dripped from beams, and turned blankets on berthing racks into sodden rags. The ship sweated as freely as the men she carried.

Jack had served for two years as a gunner on the flat-top, but he was still unused to the ship's intense heat and cramped quarters.

When the *Yorker* docked in Hawaii for supplies, refueling, and to pick up a new crew from the recently scuttled *Valor Bay*, Jack breathed a prayer of thanks to whatever deity might be listening.

Some of the crew were taking a day of liberty. Others went ashore for routine work. At least the *Yorker's* innards wouldn't be crammed with as much humanity for a few days.

As the new gunners from *Valor Bay* hoisted their gear and mounted the ramp to their new ship, Jack and his younger shipmate, Drew Brackman, spied from the deck like nosy neighbors.

The contrast in their appearance was startling.

At twenty-four, Jack moved with the easy grace of a professional dancer. Dark-haired and dark-eyed, his good looks got him noticed. The Navy regulated his life, trimmed his hair, and dictated his actions, but could do nothing about the spark of defiance in his eyes.

Drew, four years Jack's junior, was tall enough to be his buddy's shadow. His blond navy haircut gave him the look of a hatchling chick, and the muscles he'd gained on the gun crew seemed more accidental than earned.

"Just a bunch of regular guys," Jack said as they watched the last of the men from *Valor Bay* disappear into the ship.

Drew's answer lacked conviction. "I guess. Except maybe for the big one. He doesn't look real happy about life in general."

"Can't blame him," Jack said. "His ship didn't sink. It got murdered." He nudged Drew's shoulder. "Worried, Brackman? I thought you holy types weren't scared of anything."

Drew slid him an annoyed sideways glance. "The only thing I worry about is the stuff that comes out of your mouth most of the time."

Jack shrugged. "Just giving you something to pray about. I figured you'd appreciate the practice. Besides, out here, it's healthy to worry."

Drew smirked good-naturedly.

They stood together in silence for a few minutes, savoring the rare quiet.

"Eat, drink, and enjoy the dames, Brackman," Jack said after a moment, "because tomorrow you might just get blown out of the water."

They turned from the railing and made their way towards the hatch leading to the berthing compartments below.

"I thought you were done chasing dames," Drew said.

"What's it to you?"

"Nothin'," Drew said with a shrug. "Just makin' conversation. Loretta sounds like a nice girl from what you've told me. You said her kid likes you."

Jack gave him the look of a wiser sage. "Junior, your religion's wrecking you. You've got to get out in the real world more often. You've got a lot to learn."

"I'm not religious," Drew protested. "I'm—"

"Loretta's not just another dame. She's permanent. There's a difference. You'll find out what I mean someday."

He shrugged. "Anyway, doesn't matter. Shore leave's a pipe dream. If they didn't give it to me this time, it's not gonna happen anytime soon. Let's go see what we're stuck with."

They took the ladder below. Jack led the way, winding effortlessly between iron railings and thrumming machinery built so close together that even rail-thin Drew banged his elbows and bruised his shins as he hurried to keep pace.

The three fresh additions from the *Bay* were already being welcomed by their shipmates. A young sailor with a slim build was getting ribbed about his innocent appearance. Someone called him Peterson. An older guy, balding and soft around the middle, worked the room with easy confidence, introducing himself as Unger to anyone who'd listen.

The big guy, who'd already caught Jack and Drew's attention, said nothing. He was about thirty, Jack guessed. His seabag had the name *Bill Smith "Smitty"* stenciled on the side.

Smitty was too friendly a nickname for this bruiser, Jack thought. Killer or Pulverizer would have fit him in a wrestling ring.

Jack hung back to analyze. He'd learned how to read a new crew fast. Even from several paces away, this guy radiated hostility like a heater. Smitty wasn't someone you'd invite for a friendly game of chess or acey-deucey.

So, is it Valor Bay shell shock? Jack wondered. O*r just a naturally rotten temperament*?

He was so preoccupied with his analysis, he didn't realize he was being analyzed, too. The other two *Valor Bay* veterans, Unger and young Peterson, stared at him with a mixture of shock and disbelief. Peterson nudged Unger in the ribs. The older man gave him a brief nod and shot Smitty an anxious look. Jack wasn't the ghost Unger had thought, but that wasn't going to defuse things.

"It's too hot in this sardine can for the welcome wagon," Smitty complained. He prodded a few men aside. "It's not gonna get any cooler, either, so let's just pretend we're all acquainted and spread out." He adjusted the bag on his arm. "Besides, you already know who I am. Everybody's the same on every ship. Point me to my rack locker."

A few of the men exchanged glances. The expressions on some turned defensive.

"I said, what locker's mine?" Smitty barked.

"You wanna know what you can do with your locker?" someone asked.

Drew stepped up. "I think I know which one is yours. Come on, Smith, I'll show you."

"Smitty," the big man grunted. "Don't ever call me Smith."

"I'll remember," Drew said. "Come on."

Jack knew he was witnessing a modern miracle. The crew of the *New Yorker* was struck dumb for the first time in the two years he'd known them.

Smitty brushed past Jack without noticing him.

Carl Unger watched until he was sure Smitty was out of earshot, then he stepped up to Jack and said, "I'm gonna do you a favor, pal, and warn you up front." He cast an anxious glance over his shoulder.

Jack looked mystified. "Warn me about what?" He glanced at Smitty, who was still trying to find his locker with Drew's help. "You mean about your shipmate there?"

He snorted and waved Unger's concerns away. "Hey, look, don't worry. I know what happened to you guys on the *Bay*. If he's got trouble, who can blame him? We'll just give him space for a while. He'll see we're on his side."

Unger raised his eyebrows. "There's no *we* about it. It's just *you* that's gotta give him space. And he's never gonna think you're on his side, so forget that." He leaned in confidentially. "We had a gunner on the *Bay* who froze when the Zeros came in. A lot of guys died because of him. I hate to tell you this, but you look a lot like him."

Jack drew back, surprised.

Unger nodded. "Just stay out of his way. Smitty's a good man, but he doesn't need somebody up front and personal every day reminding him of what happened. He was in the tub next to Powell. One of the few who got out alive. He's not the kind to forgive and forget."

Jack gave him a skeptical look. "Come on, I can't look that much like the guy."

"Enough to fool his grandma if she wasn't lookin' close. You're not the spittin' image, but enough to give me and the Kid a good scare for a few seconds."

Jack gave Smitty a cautious glance, then looked back at Unger. "Thanks for the heads up, but take a look around. This place is shoulder-to-shoulder right now, and that's with guys on leave. Odds are we're gonna bump into each other. Besides, I've been here for two years. I think it's up to him to fit in, not the other way around."

Unger saw movement from the corner of his eye and took a few steps back. "He's comin'."

Jack turned to see Smitty returning, his bag still over his shoulder, with Drew not far behind. "The runt showed me the wrong place," Smitty grumbled. "I need to know where to park. Somebody's got to have some brains here."

He passed Jack, still without seeing him.

Jack's eyebrows ascended by degrees. Battle fatigue he could understand, but if Unger thought he was going to run and hide from Smitty like a cockroach when the lights came on, he had another think coming.

Jack got enough ribbing already from the crew about his civilian career as a dancer. He wouldn't give them even more ammunition by hiding from a threat. Besides, all the man probably needed was a friendly greeting to reassure him.

Jack came up from behind Smitty and tapped his shoulder.

Smitty turned and his face went ugly. He eyed Jack from head to toe, then glared at him with more animosity than Jack had ever seen in anyone.

Jack held up his hands. "Whoa, pal. I'm not him. Your friend here says I remind you of somebody else, but I'm not the guy." He held out his hand. "Brian Jackson. Most people call me Jack."

The *Yorker* crew exchanged curious glances.

Drew watched with growing concern. Jack could be volatile. Smitty didn't look like a peacemaker, either. *Lord, please,*" he prayed inwardly. *Get in the middle.*

Jack grasped Smitty's hand and shook it, as though it might come off if he shook hard enough. "Welcome aboard the *New Yorker*, Smitty, or as we like to call her when the captain's not listening, the tub most likely to leak in all the wrong places."

Everyone laughed, the other two *Valor Bay* newcomers included, but Smitty jerked his hand free. "Hey there, pal," he said, showing teeth in a mock grin. "Now that we're all acquainted, keep outta my way and we'll both stay outta the brig."

Jack tensed.

Drew glanced around at his shipmates. He wasn't the only one waiting for Jack to erupt.

Unger grabbed Smitty's arm from behind. The big man shook him off.

"Smitty, c'mon, don't start this," Unger said. "We're new here. If the master-at-arms is listening, you're gonna get nailed. This guy didn't do anything to you."

"Let 'em come," Smitty grunted. "Bring all the MAs you want."

He pushed roughly enough past Jack to knock him off balance.

Swell, Jack thought. *Now I've got a target on my back for trying to be friendly to a guy who oughta be in the loony bin.*

Smitty seemed oblivious to the tension he'd created. "I'll find the locker myself."

"Jackson, listen," Peterson apologized. "Give him a little time."

Jack clenched his fists at his sides without taking his slit-eyed glare off the back of Smitty's thick neck. He drew a deep breath and gave Peterson a nod. "Forget it. After that crack I made about the ship leaking after what just happened to you guys, I'm surprised he didn't cave my face in."

"Thanks," Peterson breathed, relieved.

Jack shrugged and walked as casually as his wounded pride would allow to his rack at the far end of the cabin.

A shipmate rounded on Drew. "Jackson didn't say anything! He just let that guy get away with it!"

"'Scuse me," Drew said. He meandered to Jack, who was rearranging something in his rack drawer. "Hey, Jack, what happened back there?" he said so no one else could hear.

Jack slid the door of the under-rack locker into place and stood. "What're you talking about?"

"Come on," Drew said. "You know what I'm talking about. Whatever that was all about, I thought you'd at least shoot your mouth off. That's what you usually do."

Jack's eyes widened with mock innocence. "Who, me?" He scowled and cast a glance in Smitty's direction. "Don't think it didn't cross my mind." He made a flippant gesture. "I mean, I know what those guys've been through, but it's not like I've never been in battle myself. Just 'cause the jackass had trouble doesn't mean I have to be used by him for target practice.

"Besides, I've got Loretta and the Kid to think of now. They look up to me. I don't plan to get arrested because some dope made me mad."

Drew's grin started small and spread.

"Stop staring at me like that!" Jack ordered. "And get outta my way. I've got things to do."

Drew stepped aside, careful not to grin again until Jack's back turned.

***

Carl Unger found Smitty on deck later that evening before Darken Ship. He ignored his mood. "Good to be getting back out. I know the powers that be think shore leave solves everything, but I was getting nervous. You'd think that after what happened on the *Bay*, I'd have had enough for a while."

They stood in silence for a minute. "That Jackson fella," Unger said. "You've gotta give him a break, pal. Not his fault if he looks like Powell. When you get up close, he doesn't look much like him at all."

Smitty's grunt was answer enough.

Unger folded his arms across his chest. "If anybody knows how you feel, I do. But Powell's dead, along with all the others he took out with him."

Smitty's jaw hardened. "Powell was a coward. Pretty boy. Always braggin', always mouthin' off. Better'n me, better'n everybody else. But when it mattered, he was nothin'. Because of him, good men died, and the *Bay* went down."

Unger snorted. "Powell didn't sink the *Bay* all by himself, Smit."

"He didn't do anything to save her, either."

"Come on, everybody was scared that day. You can't blame Powell for being human." He shrugged. "Or maybe you can. It doesn't make any difference now, cause Powell's dead.

"And you can't go hating an innocent man because he reminds you of somebody else. It's not right. Besides, if the master-at-arms gets wind of how you're pushing, you could land in the brig."

Smitty barely heard him. "I don't need two of that kind in one lifetime. He better stay outta my way."

Unger shook his head. "You know something, Smit? You're a hard guy to warm up to sometimes."

Smitty snorted. "Live with it."

Unger glanced toward the hatch leading below. "It's not me I'm worried about. I just hope those guys can live with it, 'cause you and me been through too much together for me not to back you. Don't put me in that kinda position."

Smitty didn't answer.

Chapter Two

Smitty laughed as Drew removed his black Bible from the berthing locker beneath his rack. "Look at Saint Andrew off to Sunday school. Don't forget your halo, Brackman. Shine it up real good so everybody can tell you're better'n the rest of us."

With one hand on the locker door and the other around the Bible, Drew stiffened at the jab. As a chaplain's aide, he attended chapel a few nights a week to lay out materials and hymnals for Bible studies.

A few guys still laughed at Smitty's digs at Jack's friend, but after two weeks, most of them were tired of it.

"Lay off the Kid," someone griped. "Part of his duty is to help the chaplain."

Drew stood and slid the locker door shut with his foot. "Chaplain Mitchell asked me to get a list of prayer requests. You got family at home you want prayed for, Smitty?"

Smitty made an obscene gesture.

"Hey, Kid," Jack called from across the room.

Drew glanced at Jack, who was playing chess with a shipmate on a lower rack across the cabin.

Jack didn't look up from the chessboard. "Do me a favor."

"What?"

"If you see the preacher tonight and he gets to the part where he tells you to forgive your enemies, give him a choice. God can either let the Japanese or Smitty through the pearly gates. If he chooses Smitty, he made the wrong choice."

Smitty bellowed. "You dirty—!"

"Your queen's in trouble," Jack informed his chess partner.

As he climbed the ladder to the hatch, Drew rolled his eyes and tucked the Bible under his arm. Smitty, never fast on the uptake, was winding up for a comeback. Drew wanted to be gone before he did.

"Jackson, you dirty dog!" Smitty yelled as Drew reached the hatch. "If you were any dumber, you'd be— "

"You?" Jack interrupted.

Drew pulled himself through. Getting away, even for an hour, was welcome.

For most of the crew, Jack and Smitty's verbal battles were a break from the anxiety of shipboard life, but Drew hated being caught in the middle.

The chapel was almost empty. Near the back, two swabbies sat on the bolted wooden pews.

"You guys here for the Bible study?" Drew asked, though he doubted it. The chapel was a popular spot for privacy during the week.

They didn't answer.

"Chaplain asked me to make up a list for prayer," Drew said. "You guys want to add anything?"

One of them gave him a sour look. "Why don't you take a long walk off a short pier, Brackman?"

Drew shrugged. "Have it your own way." He placed the study notes and hymnbooks on several pews. When he finished, he sat in the front row and closed his eyes.

A few minutes later, he heard the men leave.

Drew opened his eyes. "We might not even be alive tomorrow," he muttered. "You'd think they'd care more about what comes after this."

It's better to whistle past the graveyard, Brackman, he remembered Jack saying, *than stop and think about being in one of the graves.*

Drew sighed. He and Jack could talk about almost anything unless it was Drew's faith. Their philosophies of life were point, counterpoint, yet they clicked on a level Drew didn't understand.

A soft cough near the door caused him to look up.

Chaplain Mitchell stood in the doorway.

The chaplain was just leaving his youth behind. He had dark hair going gray on the sides. His eyes had the beginning of crow's feet, and his expression, whether by nature or practice, was always sympathetic.

Drew started to rise.

Mitchell motioned him down. "No, stay there. Mind if I join you?"

"Of course not, sir." He made a sweeping gesture at the empty chapel. "Plenty of seats. Take your pick."

Mitchell snorted with amusement and sat beside him.

Drew handed him the prayer list. "Not much there. The guys don't like to talk to me about stuff like this."

Mitchell took the list and gave it a cursory glance. "Hm. Well, that's because you're one of them. They don't want to look weak."

He laid the list aside on the pew and said, "Don't let it bother you. They come to me and the other chaplains for prayer and counseling during the week. Most are scared. Some just need reassurance that God's there."

Drew nodded. "I know. I thought getting chapel duty might give me a chance to pray or talk with some of them. Seems like all I do, though, is put paper and books on empty pews."

"Not true," Mitchell protested. "You pass out communion on Sundays."

"That's important, but I wish the Lord would use me to do more. I want to tell them what it means. They don't listen to me."

Mitchell nodded. "Listen, I've got something to discuss with you. You said you'd already enrolled in seminary when the war hit."

Drew nodded. "Just a few days before."

"Not the best timing," Mitchell sympathized. "I know your views, and I've read your statement of faith. I'd like to talk to the Captain about giving you more responsibility as my aide. Maybe then your shipmates will recognize you as someone they can open up to."

Drew looked doubtful. "I'd like to do that, Chaplain, but I wouldn't count on anyone telling me any secrets."

"All we can do is try. I'd also like you to lead the midweek Bible studies."

"I can do that."

Mitchell smiled. "Who knows. Maybe you'll decide to become a Navy chaplain after the war."

Drew laughed. "I don't think so, sir. I'm going home to Dorrie. We're gonna be the best team outside Manhattan that the Lord ever put together." He shrugged. "Of course, like Dorrie always says, never say never. I'll just wait to see what the Lord has in mind."

***

In the crowded mess cabin, Drew sat at the long table bolted to the deck among dozens of other men forced to sit shoulder to shoulder as they ate.

Smitty and his *Valor Bay* shipmates sat near the middle of the table because the far end was taken.

"So, you're like a chaplain now?" Jack asked Drew. He forked an unidentifiable mass on his plate and held it up for Drew's inspection. "Maybe you should pray about this."

"I don't even know what that is. How can I pray for it?"

Eying the mystery on his fork, Jack took a cautious bite.

Drew watched his reaction. "Well?"

Jack chewed. "I think it's meatloaf." Then nodding, he gave his approval. "Some kind of meat. I don't think it's dangerous."

Laughing, the gunner sitting next to Jack nudged his shoulder. "It's too bad when you have to wonder if your food is more dangerous than the enemy, eh, Jackson?" He took a bite, gave an approving nod, and speared another chunk.

"So, what's the deal?" Jack said to Drew. "You're a chaplain now?"

"Not by a long shot," Drew snorted. "I'm just there to help the chaplain pray with guys who ask for it. Help a little with Bible studies. You know, like that."

"Sweet gig," Jack said. "I've got ordnance and mechanics duty." He gave a rueful sigh. "My fault. They offered me a position in the entertainment division, but I turned it down."

"When do we get a show outta ya, Jackson?" someone asked.

Jack didn't look up from his plate. "Need money first."

"So much for brotherly love," the man grinned. "So, why'd you turn down entertainment duty?"

"Why do you think?"

"Because he's always got to make sure he's in the middle of all the action," the sailor on Jack's left suggested.

"Yeah, and I oughta get the dope of the century award," Jack said. "You know, it's one thing to get all patriotic and believe you're gonna save the world before you enlist. It's a whole 'nother ball game when you actually get here."

"That's part of what my job is supposed to be," Drew said. "Chaplain says a lot of guys come to him who have a hard time with it all." He glanced around the crowded mess cabin at the men, laughing and talking with one another as they ate. "You'd never think to look at 'em, would ya?"

"What about you, Brackman?" someone asked. "You adjusted yet?"

Drew snorted. "Yeah, I'm real adjusted to shooting people I don't know and watching my friends get blown to smithereens."

"So, what makes you fit to give advice?" another sailor asked, without malice.

"Well," Drew said. "I guess I've been here longer than some of 'em, so I'm more—what's the word I'm looking for?"

"Seasoned," Jack volunteered.

"I guess," Drew said.

"You look like a kid just outta high school," someone else said.

Drew glanced at Jack. "Not like this blowhard, who spent his whole life on stage."

"I got educated on the road," Jack said. He reached for a biscuit. "So, besides being seasoned, what other credentials you got?"

"Don't ask him that," Smitty grumbled. "He'll preach the gospel."

Drew didn't take offense. "Nothing wrong with the gospel." He took another bite. "I'm not gonna apologize."

Jack pushed his plate away and leaned forward. "None of it makes sense to me. How does letting yourself get beat up and put on a cross do anybody any good?"

"It was a rescue mission," Drew said. "He paid the price."

"What's that supposed to mean?" someone asked.

Drew paused, studying Jack's cynical expression. Then something clicked. He had the perfect analogy for a man who understood theater. "Okay, let's say somebody offers to give you a free ticket to a Broadway show."

"Yeah, all right," Jack said.

"The guy who gives you the ticket bought and paid for it," Drew went on. "You can go into the show, but first you have to believe the ticket's legit, then you have to take it. It's up to you. You can take the ticket or turn it down. If you turn it down, you've got no right to complain about missing the show."

"Huh!" someone exclaimed. "I never thought about it like that before. That's pretty good, Brackman."

Mealtime was up, and the men dispersed to their assigned duties.

As they left the hall, Jack said, "They put you in the right job, Brackman."

"Thanks," Drew said.

Chapter Three

New York, Manhattan, January 1943

Drew's letter had become almost too wrinkled to read. It had faded in places where Dorrie Martin had read and re-read his most endearing passages.

To make sure she didn't mess up the part about Loretta Truett, Jack's girl, she left the letter at home and looked up the address in the directory.

Impulsively, on her way to work that morning, she found the place. After work, she planned to come back and introduce herself to Loretta.

Now she stood on the sidewalk in front of a sandstone Manhattan townhouse, wondering if she had the right address. There had been only one Loretta Truett in the phone book.

The house's bay windows with lace curtains looked like a picture in a magazine. Everything about the place was so perfect, so clean. It looked brand new. It wasn't the type of place she'd expected to find as home for the girl of one of Drew's shipmates.

The weather was warm for January. Dorrie wore a light cloth coat, unbuttoned, over her pink cotton waitress uniform with a name tag that read *Dorrie*. The matching apron with pockets and comfortable white shoes completed her uniform, but seemed almost an insult to the neighborhood.

Drew had said nothing about Loretta's being rich.

She was about to leave when the front door opened. A young woman stepped out, holding the hand of a red-headed boy who looked about six.

Now Dorrie was sure she was in the wrong place. This person couldn't be Brian Jackson's girlfriend, could she?

The woman could have stepped out of a movie screen. She was young and beautiful, with sculpted cheekbones brushed in rose-colored blush. Long auburn hair tumbled across the shoulders of her cream wool suit with fitted jacket and pencil skirt. The outfit framed her figure with an elegance Dorrie had only seen in magazines.

The little boy's tweed suit and matching cap didn't look so shabby, either, Dorrie thought. He didn't dress like the kids on her block. They often wore rumpled trousers and scuffed shoes from playing stickball in the streets.

The beautiful woman acknowledged Dorrie's existence with a smile as she came down the last step. "Hello there. Lovely day, isn't it?"

Dorrie was about to let her walk away, but then she figured the lady couldn't shoot her for asking a few questions. "Excuse me, ma'am," she called.

The woman kept walking. She raised her hand as a Checker Cab approached from down the street.

Dorrie tried again. "Excuse me, ma'am!"

The lady stopped and looked back. "I'm sorry. Are you talking to me?"

"Hang on a second, will ya?" Dorrie hoped the lady didn't think she wanted a handout.

She trotted toward her, gathered her courage, and said, "Is there any chance ya might be Loretta Truett?" She looked down at the child and waved. "Hi, kiddo!"

The little boy waved back.

The pretty woman gave her a curious look. "Why do you ask?"

The driver rolled down the passenger-side window and said, "Are you the one who called for a cab?"

"Yes, I am," the lady said. "Can you hang on for just a moment? I'll pay extra." She turned back to Dorrie. "What can I do for you?"

Uncomfortable, Dorrie shifted her weight. Up close, the woman's beauty was like seeing a statue come to life. "Actually," she said, "I just wanna know if ya know someone by the name of Brian Jackson."

The woman's hand flew to her chest. "Jack? You know Jack?" She grasped Dorrie's shoulder. "Is he all right? Has anything happened to him?"

Well, what do ya know? Dorrie thought. *She is the one!*

Dorrie patted her hand. "Calm down, he's okay, far as I know. At least he was in the last letter I got from Drew about a month ago. Anyway, I'm sorry. I didn't mean to scare ya." She clasped the woman's hand in a handshake. "My name's Dorrie Martin. I'm Drew's intended."

Loretta's nose wrinkled. "His intended what?"

"We're gonna get married."

"Oh! I'm sorry. I don't know anyone named Drew."

"Sure, ya do!" Dorrie exclaimed. "Drew Brackman. He's Jack's buddy on the *New Yorker*. Didn't Jack ever mention him when he wrote to ya?"

Loretta's mouth formed an enlightened oval. "Oh, *that* Drew!"

"Lady?" the cab driver asked.

"Oh," Loretta said. "Oh, I'm sorry." She reached into her purse, extracted a few bills, and handed them to the driver. "I'm sorry, you can go on, I'll call for another cab." She turned back to Dorrie. "This is wonderful! How nice to meet you!"

Dorrie felt her anxiety ebb. The goddess seemed to be pretty nice. "Drew said that ya live in Manhattan. I'm from Mount Vernon, myself, and that's not so far, so I—"

"How did you find me?"

"Phone book."

"Am I still listed? Well, this is one time I'm glad of it. How nice you tracked me down!" She indicated Dorrie's name tag. "That's a Kress tag. I'd recognize it anywhere."

A blush of embarrassment rose in Dorrie's face. "Sometimes I kinda work there."

"And your name is Dorrie, I see."

The little boy fidgeted and tugged at Loretta's hand. "Mommy, let's go!"

Loretta jiggled his hand. "In a minute, darling." She looked back at Dorrie. "This is my son, Russell."

Dorrie stooped to his level. "Hi, Russell. Does anybody ever call ya Rusty?"

Russell nodded. "Uncle Jack does, but Mommy said people should call me Russell."

"Well, mommies know best," Dorrie said. She resisted the urge to ruffle his hair. "Drew didn't mention that Jack had a little boy," she said as she straightened.

"Jack doesn't," Loretta said. "Russell is *my* son."

Dorrie nodded. "Oh, sure. You and Jack are just engaged."

"I'm sorry, Dorrie," Loretta apologized, "but I'm already late for work and I still have to drop Russell at school. Maybe if you come by this evening, we can have tea and talk."

"Sure, I'd like that," Dorrie said. She wouldn't have missed seeing the inside of that townhouse for anything. "Is five o'clock too early? I know that's around supper time."

"Five o'clock works perfectly."

"There's another cab coming," Dorrie said, pointing.

Loretta raised a hand to hail the car. She bundled Russell into the back seat and climbed in beside him.

Dorrie waved as the car pulled away. She glanced back at the townhouse and shook her head. "Whoever woulda thought?"

***

Dorrie got off work at three and took the commuter train from Grand Central to her one-bedroom apartment in Mount Vernon. She changed into her best plaid skirt and white blouse with ruffles down the front and pulled on black flats.

She briefly considered applying powder and blush to look more *cosmopolitan*, as the magazines called it. But why bother? She'd never be able to compete in the glamour department with Loretta Truett. It didn't matter, anyway. Drew liked her the way she was.

She took the commuter train back to Manhattan and walked the extra ten minutes to Loretta's house.

Loretta opened the door. She wore a loose polka-dot sweater, casual high-waisted trousers, and brown loafers. A ponytail held back her thick auburn hair.

She still looked prettier than most, Dorrie thought, but dressed down, she was less intimidating.

"Come in," Loretta smiled, holding the door open. "I hope you like crumb cake because I spent an hour putting one together in your honor." She made a wry face. "Of course, no one can get coffee these days, darn it. No guarantees on how the cake tastes, either. I've never made one before."

Dorrie laughed. "Thanks! I've never had a cake just for me before, except for birthday cake. Where's Rusty?"

"I shooed him out with his nanny. I wanted us to sit and talk without being interrupted. We can't do that with him chattering. They'll be gone for a little while. Come on in."

Dorrie stepped in and glanced as casually as her curiosity would allow at the surroundings, trying not to make her interest too obvious.

The foyer inside the door had black and white tile flooring and a crystal chandelier that reminded her of the top of the Empire State Building.

The parlor was more traditional. It had ceilings so high Dorrie had to crane her neck to see the top. The wallpaper was silk with Chinese floral accents. A gleaming black baby grand piano at the far side of the room completed the elegant scene.

Loretta motioned to the couch. "Excuse the mess. I'm redesigning. My ex-husband was obsessed with Art Deco. His era, not mine."

Dorrie glanced around. "It's beautiful. Just like a hotel."

Loretta laughed. "That's what I thought when I saw it the first time, too. It's a little intimidating, I know. Sit down. Make yourself comfortable."

Dorrie expected Loretta's next words to be *I'll ring for tea*, but she said, "Let me go get the cake and stuff. I'll be back in a jiff! If you're curious, Jack's picture is on top of the piano."

While Loretta went for refreshments, Dorrie wandered over to investigate Drew's best pal. Jack appeared to be in his mid-twenties, strikingly handsome, but not innocent-looking. Something in his eyes said he'd lived through things, and his grin promised trouble if challenged.

Dorrie was surprised. She'd always thought Jack would look more like Drew.

Loretta returned with tea and cake.

"Jack's handsome," Dorrie said. She sat on the sofa beside Loretta.

Loretta gave her a knowing look. "And he knows it, too. Do you have a picture of Drew that I can see?"

"Right here." Dorrie dug into her purse and withdrew the picture of her boyfriend from her wallet.

"Oh, look at him, what a doll! Like a sweet little boy. Cream and sugar?"

Dorrie was startled. Drew was a gunner on an aircraft carrier, not a child. "Drew's a good man," she said. "He's gonna be a minister when he comes home. I'll take two lumps, thanks."

Loretta laughed. "No kidding? I can't imagine Jack being friends with anyone religious. How'd they end up being friendly?"

"Drew says they look out for each other," Dorrie said and changed the subject. "How'd you make a real cake? I can't get butter and eggs to save me."

"I have a few friends in the restaurant business. They throw me a crumb now and then." She chuckled. "Look at that, I made a joke without even trying." She stirred her tea. "My ex-husband has lots of contacts. Some of them still feel sorry for Russell and me for what he did to us."

Dorrie was almost afraid to ask. "What did he do?"

"He divorced me when he found out I was expecting. You may have heard of him. Moe Truett?"

Dorrie shook her head.

"Just as well," Loretta said. "A rat. He owns almost everybody in theater." She hesitated. "Not Jack, though. Nobody owns Jack. Sometimes I wonder if even I do."

"I'm sorry to hear ya had such a hard time," Dorrie said. "Sounds like ya got a good guy in Jack, though. What's he like?"

Loretta settled back against the couch cushion. "Oh, my, that could take all afternoon. Let's see. He's good-looking and sarcastic, not in a mean way, just enough to be cute. He started in vaudeville with his folks."

"Gee," Dorrie exclaimed.

Loretta nodded. "Scouts picked him up early, but he still had to work for years to get real recognition. It paid off, though. He finally headlined a show at the Belmont Theater just before the war."

"Is he an actor?"

"Oh yes, and a good one, but his real talent is dancing. Now then, let me hear a little something about you."

Dorrie sipped her tea. "Not much to tell. I teach first-grade Sunday School and play on the church softball team. I'm the pitcher. I go to secretary school at night. I can't work the breakfast counter at Kress forever, ya know!"

Loretta laughed.

"That's me in a nutshell," Dorrie said. "What do you do in your spare time?"

"What spare time? After Moe, I didn't want to just sit around. I couldn't do any acting for reasons I don't need to go into. I'm fairly attractive, so I called my folks' old manager. He got me some modeling gigs. That's what I do now."

"Well, that makes sense," Dorrie said. "You're prettier'n most. That's what ya should be doin'."

"Aw, you're sweet," Loretta said. "*Marquee Quarterly* magazine is putting me on the cover this week. That should give me tons of exposure. I was on my way to a photo shoot this morning when we bumped into one another."

Dorrie felt embarrassed. "Makes me goin' to night school sound pretty boring."

Loretta patted her arm. "Don't be silly. You've got a good heart, I can tell, and that's worth a lot in this rotten world. We need ordinary people to get us through."

Dorrie wasn't sure if she'd just received a compliment or an insult, but she nodded. "I guess."

"I'm glad you came," Loretta said. "Let me cut you another slice. You deserve to be spoiled once in a while, too."

When Dorrie left, Loretta watched from the window as she walked away. *Poor little* thing, she thought. *She and that boy don't stand a chance. A minister, of all things*!

She had to write to Jack.

Chapter Four

Russell Truett didn't know what his mother did all day. It somehow involved lots of red lipstick, pretty clothes that sparkled, and what she called 'horrible hot lights,' whatever that meant.

But he knew what *he* was good at: telling Uncle Jack stories. He thought them up at night when his mother thought he was asleep. He acted them out so he could tell them just right. At recess, the playground behind the school became his stage.

Today, Russell had a brand-new story to tell.

Almost all the children in his first-grade class at the Dwight School in the Upper West Side of Manhattan knew someone fighting in the war, but Russell's stories about the sailor he knew made all the other stories seem dull.

Russell's Uncle Jack became a symbol of every father, uncle, or brother they knew fighting so far away.

"Uncle Jack lives on a great big ship called the *New Yorker*," he began, as always. Russell stood on top of a wooden picnic table while the other boys and girls sat around it, or on swings, monkey bars, and the red, white, and blue-painted roundabout.

"It's a great big ship with airplanes on it," Russell continued. "The planes just sit there until bad guys come, and when they do, Uncle Jack tells the people in the airplanes to fly off the ship and get 'em. Uncle Jack is the boss, even more than the Admiral."

He spread his arms like a plane and ran around the top of the table, mimicking the sound of an airplane engine.

With his aerial performance complete, he returned to the story.

"Uncle Jack's other job is to shoot his guns at the bad guys." He pointed both fingers like machine guns. "Rat-tat-tat! Pow! Pow!"

"We know, we know," a little girl on the wooden roundabout complained. "You told us this the last time!" She bounced impatiently on her knees, causing the roundabout to shift on its axle.

The few children who sat there hung on, but after a lazy half-turn, the carousel stopped.

"Okay, okay," Russell conceded. "Now, I'm going to tell you a new story." He chewed his bottom lip, thinking. He'd already spent hours crafting the story in his head, but it needed something more. His eyes brightened.

"Now, on this one day," he said. "Uncle Jack was walking up and down on the deck of the ship—that's what they call the floor on a ship in the Navy. He was looking out at the water with his binoculars to see if any bad guys were coming, but he didn't see any." Russell gave the children a knowing look. "That was because the bad guys knew Uncle Jack was on the ship, and they were scared of him."

The children nodded.

"Uncle Jack said to the Admiral, I think it's okay if you take a break, sir. Even if you're the boss like Jack, you have to call the Admiral sir. It's a special rule."

"Everybody knows that," a boy with a father in the Navy scoffed.

Russell ignored him. "Jack told the Admiral that he needed to go ashore. That means leave the boat and go on vacation, like I said.

"So, the Admiral went ashore. Uncle Jack drove the ship away. Of course, he would come back later and pick the Admiral up again, but not right now because he didn't want the Admiral to come back until his vacation was over.

"When the Admiral was gone, Uncle Jack showed all the other sailors how to tell the difference between a bad guy plane and an American plane, because when you're in the Navy, you ought to know.

"Well, wouldn't you know it? Just when the Admiral left, the bad guys came. They had a whole lot of airplanes, too—a lot more than the airplanes on the *New Yorker*. Those big, fast airplanes were painted all black and ugly."

There were a few expectant gasps. The little girl on the round-about clasped her hands, but she was careful not to bounce again.

"Some of the bad guys went back because they saw Uncle Jack standing on the deck with his binoculars," Russell continued. "They knew they were in big trouble.

"But Uncle Jack said, Oh no, you don't! He waved his arms and said, Go get 'em, boys! Don't let any of 'em get away! But, those bad guys were real fast!

"Uncle Jack saw that it was up to him. He got into his own special airplane, the one the Navy made 'specially for him, and he took his big gun with him.

"That really scared the bad guys, but they figured if they could shoot Uncle Jack's airplane down, then he would never bother them again, and then they could win the war."

"They can't win the war!" a terrified boy cried. "If they do, the bad guys will come here and get us!"

"That's right," Russell replied with a sage nod. "But Uncle Jack took care of 'em, so don't worry. He flew his airplane right at 'em. He wasn't even scared. He shot some of the airplanes down with his big gun, and he bumped his airplane into some of them, too, and made them crash into the water.

"Then the airplane guys from the *New Yorker* came and helped him. Pretty soon, all of the bad guys had crashed in the water, or they turned around and flew back home again."

A collective cheer went up from the children.

"I bet my daddy was in one of the airplanes that helped him!" the boy who'd chided him exclaimed.

Russell fed him a crumb. "He was. Your daddy was there, too."

The little boy jumped up and down. "My daddy helped Uncle Jack!"

"Then what happened?" someone asked.

"Then Uncle Jack went back and picked up the Admiral," Russell said. "And guess what? The Admiral gave Uncle Jack a medal, and guess what, too? Uncle Jack said when he comes home, he's gonna give the medal to me."

"Did the Admiral give my daddy a medal, too?" the boy asked.

"Yes, he did," Russell allowed, "but not as big as Uncle Jack's medal because Uncle Jack is the boss."

The school bell rang, and recess ended. The children returned to class.

Russell couldn't concentrate on silly things like spelling and reading. He was already thinking up his next Uncle Jack story.

Somewhere in the fog, he heard his teacher's voice through his daydream. "Mr. Truett, are you with us?"

The children giggled.

Russell looked up, startled.

The teacher smiled. "Were you daydreaming?"

Russell sat up in his chair and nodded. "Yes," he said. "I was thinking about Uncle Jack."

Chapter Five

Jack rubbed his hands together, a predatory gleam in his eyes.

"One day to crossing," he grinned. His eagerness tipped toward something maniacal. "This morning, the inquisition. This afternoon, we feast on the lowliest wogs to ever disgrace a ship since time began."

Drew regarded him cautiously.

Jack whooped. "Three officers! Think of it, Brackman! We not only got a hundred wogs to roast, but we got three whole officers to torture, too, and there's not a thing they can do about it!"

His grin dropped into a momentary scowl. "Too bad Smitty's not a wog, but you can't have everything, right?"

Jack slung an arm around Drew's shoulders before he could answer. "I've been elected Neptune by the whole ship. I'm making you my official notetaker. Consider yourself grateful."

Uncertainty twisted Drew's features. "Uh, Jack?"

"You wouldn't believe the horrors I've come up with," Jack chortled, the maniacal look back in his eyes. "If any of these guys survive, they'll be talkin' about this for years. Forget the Japanese. When these wogs start telling their grandkids war stories, it's Jackson they'll remember."

Dressed in drawstring pants with towels slung across their shoulders, they made their way down the corridor toward the showers.

"What kinda horrors you got in mind, Jack?"

"Oh, you know, the usual kind, only with a Jackson twist."

"Hail, mighty Neptune!" a shipmate greeted Jack as he stepped out of the shower. "Watch out for the slime against the wall, oh great god of the briny depths. I slipped on it and nearly broke my neck."

Jack peered into the stall. "That's not slime. That's a wog if I ever saw one!"

The sailor roared with laughter, slapped Jack's bare shoulder, and walked off, drying his hair with a towel and chortling with the same insane glee that Jack had all morning.

Drew stepped into the shower and turned on the water. "When's all this torture supposed to happen?"

Jack put his head under the semi-steady trickle. "What?"

"I said," Drew hollered back, "What time's all this torture gonna happen today, anyway?"

"Hey, be careful, Brackman," a passing sailor warned, "you might go down the drain."

Drew scowled. "Ha, ha. Jack, when's the torture?"

"What's the matter with you? You've never been to a wog roast before?" Jack hollered back, the last few words gargled as he stuck his face under the water. "The inquisition starts after mess this morning."

Drew gave a solitary nod. "Oh."

"The same wiseacres who voted me Neptune thought it would be funny to make Smitty the Davy Jones Chief High Inquisitor, so I gotta look at his ugly face through the whole thing, but it's worth it."

"How come?"

Jack squinted, blinking water out of his eyes. "What're you asking me all these questions for? If a guy didn't know better, he'd think you'd never crossed the equator before."

Drew looked at him, hopelessness growing in his eyes.

Jack's face blanked. "You're kidding."

Drew's mouth twisted to one side. He shrugged a bony shoulder.

Jack shut off the water. "Aw, c'mon, Brackman, you're joking."

"Nope. I came to the ship by air after ammunition school, so I never got the chance."

"C'mon already," a sailor waiting outside the shower room barked. "You finished in there or what? There's a million guys waitin', Jackson."

Jack grabbed a towel and slung it around his waist, ignoring the impatient sailor as he pushed past him. He grabbed Drew's arm, pulling him out of the stall. "You can't be saying you never crossed The Line before."

Drew grabbed a towel. The cloth went around nearly twice. "Well, like I said, I flew in from the States after ammunition school, so—"

"So, you're a wog."

Drew nodded. "Yeah, I guess."

Jack stared at him, then smirked and swaggered towards the berthing compartment. "So, Brackman's a wog."

"So, what?" Drew protested. "The equator's not even a real line. It's not even there, Jack."

Jack stopped walking so fast Drew bumped into him. "Watch who you're calling Jack. It's Exalted High Majesty of the Sea to you."

"Aw, Jack."

"You're sunk, wog. Torpedoed." Jack grinned over his shoulder as he walked away.

"It's just a gag, right?" Drew called after him.

Jack's eyebrows went up. His eyes widened.

"Right?" Drew asked again, a note of hopelessness in his voice. He gave a deep sigh and sank onto the edge of his rack.

"All I can say," Jack's voice said over his shoulder, making him jump, "is it's a good thing you're a praying man."

***

Jack chuckled. His own wog initiation had occurred six months into his tenure aboard *New Yorker.* The ritual not only relieved stress but was also great fun, although every uninitiated pollywog was made to believe it was hell on earth.

The pranks weren't as bad as every seasoned man on board, the shellbacks, made them sound.

The most extreme prank Jack had heard of was when the Board of Inquisitors ordered a man to spend the whole day saluting as many inanimate objects in the crowded quarters as he could.

When Jack finally took his exalted Neptunian throne, a wooden folding chair on top of a long dining table in the Officer's Mess, Smitty took his place beside him.

Smitty surprised Jack by consulting with him once or twice about the sentencing of some unfortunate wog.

By the time two hours had passed, Jack and Smitty had some wogs on deck crowing like roosters or oinking like pigs, another embroidering a map of the U.S. on his shorts.

They ordered Smitty's young pal, Peterson, to sing the first stanza of the Navy Hymn backward until he got it right while painting his face with engine grease.

Being Neptune was a tough job, Jack thought with glee, but somebody had to do it.

As long as battle stations weren't called, the inquisition and sentences would go on until late afternoon.

Smitty boomed the name of the next initiate. "Gunner's Mate Third Class Andrew Brackman, Your Highness! Been aboard for a year-and-a-half and still ain't crossed the equator!"

Boos and hisses went up, hoots and insults. Drew, proud, straight, and as dignified as any condemned man could be, stepped before the throne.

Jack stood, peered imperiously down his nose, and squared his shoulders. "So, Brackman, you've actually got the guts to stand here in this court and admit you've never crossed The Line?"

Drew grinned. "What Line?"

Cries of outrage erupted. "Hang him by his thumbs! Feed him to the sharks! Make him eat the cook's meatloaf!"

Smitty leaned toward Jack but made sure his voice carried to everyone. "This lowly wog, oh Great Neptune, has the nerve to call himself the Great King of the Sea's best pal."

Jack snorted. "Ha! Add slander to the list of charges."

"This lowly wog deserves special punishment for insulting the King of the Sea!" Smitty boomed.

Cries of agreement went up.

Jack's warning bells went off. In a flash of insight, he understood why his nemesis had been so friendly all evening.

He glared at Smitty and saw smug anticipation in the man's eyes.

"I've already planned this wog's punishment," Jack said. He stood and crossed his arms, glaring down at Drew. "For insulting the Great King Neptune by claiming to be his friend, and for never crossing The Line, I sentence you to take these binoculars"—Jack produced two tin cans strung together with wire—"and from now until we say so, sight for enemy activity."

Drew saluted sharply. "Aye, sir!"

Smitty stepped to the edge of the table. "The Great King Neptune is letting this wog off too easy! Makes you kind of wonder if they weren't pals all along, don't it?"

Smitty smirked, then grinned down at Drew. "All right, wog, here's how it goes. You do just like the Great King of the Sea told ya, but besides that, find a jacket and wear it the rest of the day."

Alarmed, Jack looked around and saw a few guys in the crowd glancing at one another.

Drew played along. "Aye-aye, sir! And if I can find gloves and a hat, I'll wear those, too." He whirled on his heel to fulfill his sentence.

Jack shot to his feet, all pretense evaporated. He jumped off the table and grabbed Drew's arm. "All right, scratch that. The coolest spot on this ship right now is a hundred and two degrees. We're not out to hurt anybody."

"Well," Smitty shrugged. "If this lowdown wog gets too hot, sir, he can just jump in the ocean for a little swim. I can see to that myself, personal-like, sir."

There wasn't as much laughter as before.

"Oh, great Neptune," Drew shouted. "Far be it from this lowly wog to back out when none of the others did!" He leaned toward Jack with a scowl and said in a voice that only he could hear, "Drop it, already."

Jack was about to make another protest when the next wog came forward.

Someone handed Drew the tin-can binoculars, and someone else pushed through the crowd to hand him a jacket. They carted him off to the sound of boos, hisses, and good-natured laughter.

Jack sat back on his throne, but as he sentenced the next wog and the next, the fun had gone out of the game.

"Don't worry about that scrawny friend of yours," Smitty leaned over to whisper. "He ain't got nothin' to sweat off, and he sure ain't got the guts to back out."

Jack's eyes narrowed. "Next time you wanna get at me, you coward, do it direct. Your time's coming, bud. Count on it."

"I'm shivering, Jackson. Shakin' in my boots."

The next lowly wog stepped forward.

As he fulfilled his sentence, Drew stayed away from Jack. The protective big brother thing could be embarrassing sometimes.

Occasionally, a shellback would rip off Drew's jacket, feigning harassment as part of the game, but Smitty was always there to make sure the coat went right back on.

The sentences continued until mid-afternoon. The final trial for each wog was a knees and elbows crawl through wet oatmeal.

Drew, still wearing the jacket, emerged triumphant, so caked in oatmeal that he was unrecognizable. He threw his fist into the air with a triumphant cry.

The shellbacks, sliding in the mess, descended on him with back-slaps and wild whoops. Someone stripped the jacket off him and gave him a hefty shove, sending him slipping back into the goo onto his backside.

Drew peered up, expecting to see Smitty. But it was Jack, grinning down at him with a triumphant thumbs-up.

***

Drew finished washing and towel-drying the last of the oatmeal out of his hair. Even with his short hair, enough of the goo had invaded his scalp and pores to make cleaning up a challenge.

The Captain ordered extra water that day for the new shellbacks and the cleanup crew.

Drew chuckled. It certainly gave the phrase 'swabbing the deck' a new meaning.

"Well, you made it," Jack grinned as Drew stepped out of the stall, still towel-drying his scalp.

"No thanks to you, Neptune," Drew grumbled amiably.

"I thought I gave you a pretty light sentence," Jack protested. As they entered the berth area, he cast a glare in Smitty's direction. "Not like that schmuck who tried to broil you alive in that jacket."

"Oh, yeah!" Drew exclaimed. "You just reminded me! I've got a thing or two to say to him."

Jack rocked back on his heels with a smug grin. "About time. Give him my regards."

Drew walked across the cabin to where Smitty sat on his bunk. Unger and Peterson sat on either side of him.

"Smit," Drew said.

Smitty looked up as he approached, his expression automatically defensive.

Drew grinned. "That was the most fun I've had since I left home. I just wanted to say thanks for making it a challenge. It wouldn't have been as good without you adding the jacket."

He didn't bother to hold out his hand because he knew Smitty wouldn't shake it. But as he turned to walk back towards Jack, he caught a glimpse from the corner of his eye of the three *Valor Bay* crew staring after him, bug-eyed and slack-jawed.

"What did you say to him?" Jack grinned. "Whatever it was, it must have been good. He looks like he just got punched."

"I said thanks," Drew said.

Jack's face blanked. "Come again?"

Drew nudged him out of the way. "Tin cans with wire. Did you stay up all night thinking up that one, genius?"

Flabbergasted, Jack stared after him before following. "Hey! I was protecting you! Do I get any thanks?"

Drew looked over his shoulder without stopping. "Thanks."

"What's wrong with you, Brackman? You don't say thanks to pond scum like Smitty!"

"I just did," Drew said. "It was worth it to see the surprise on his face, too. Besides, I meant it."

Jack's look of shock mirrored the one the *Valor Bay* trio had given him.

Sometimes, Lord, Drew sighed inwardly, *life can be so good!*

Chapter Six

The deck guns were deadly, but vulnerable. Without care, the harsh realities of saltwater, corrosion, and frequent use rendered them ineffective.

When Drew wasn't needed for chapel duty, he and Jack were among the teams that kept the cannons in shape. It was the minutes, sometimes hours, they'd worked together that cemented their friendship, making them the unlikeliest best mates on the ship.

Today, though, Jack was working with the ordnance crew further down deck. To his surprise, he had instincts for the work and enjoyed it. Before joining the Navy, his greatest skill had been executing a Maxie Ford shuffle step.

Drew was paired instead with Smitty's *Valor Bay* shipmate, Tom Peterson.

Peterson seemed like a nice enough guy, Drew thought as they worked. His loyalty to Smitty was understandable, given what they'd gone through on *Valor Bay.* Neither Peterson nor Unger ever harassed Jack the way Smitty did.

Under different circumstances, Drew thought he and Peterson could be friends. For one thing, they were the same age. The four-year difference between him and Jack sometimes seemed like decades.

After an awkward, cursory nod, he and Peterson began on the guns. For several minutes, they worked wordlessly, wiping down the grime and salt on the exterior of the first gun. Next, they cleaned the barrel with a rag and a cleaning rod. By the time they started lubricating the breech mechanisms and hinges, Drew couldn't take the silence anymore.

"Where are you from?" he asked when they moved to the next cannon.

Startled that Drew spoke to him, Peterson's head snapped up. "Uh," he said. "I'm from Silver Spring, Maryland, on the East Coast."

"I'm on the East Coast too," Drew said. "Grew up in Yonkers, just outside Manhattan."

"Oh," Peterson said. There was more silence, then Peterson asked, "You like being a chaplain's assistant?"

"It's great," Drew answered. "When I graduated from high school, I wasn't sure what I wanted to do for a living. I messed around for a while, you know?"

Peterson nodded. "I get that."

"But I've been a Christian since I was a kid, and there's nothing I like to do more than talk about Jesus, so I figured I'd enroll in seminary. I was getting the wheels rolling when Pearl was hit."

Peterson's eyes stung from sweat. He swiped his forehead with his sleeve. "How about I do the outsides, and you work on the grease?"

Drew nodded. "Okay. What about you? What're your plans after the war?"

"I haven't figured it out yet. I was working at my dad's place. He's a druggist."

"You gonna be a druggist, then?"

"Nah, it's not something I wanna do. I was just helping the old man out."

"Does he mind? That you don't want to be a druggist, I mean?"

"I don't think he wants to be a druggist, either!"

They laughed.

"You like Glenn Miller?" Peterson asked.

Drew's eyes lit. "Oh, man! That clarinet section lays it down!" He drew a straight line in the air with his gloved hand. "Smoooooth."

Peterson slapped the cannon's top. "No doubt about it, Jake!"

Drew was in his element. "But Benny Goodman's the one who really grabs me when the band plays "Sing, Sing, Sing"!"

"Yeah!" Peterson agreed. "Man, have you ever heard anything like those drums? That cat swings!"

"I know! It's like Gene Krupa's from a whole 'nother planet!"

They continued to laugh and talk as they worked, finding they had more things in common.

"I'm getting married when I get home," Drew said.

"No foolin'? What's she like?"

Drew laughed. "She's funny. She says things that make me go whaaat?" He polished the gun absent-mindedly, picturing Dorrie in his mind. "She doesn't try to impress anybody. She's just who she is. How 'bout you?"

"Not yet. Gonna sow some wild oats before I settle down. I want to have some fun first, after this nightmare is over, you know? Where'd you meet your girl?"

"Church. Well, no, that's not right. I saw her in high school first, but we really didn't get to know each other until later when we started going to the same church."

Peterson snorted. "Figures." He was quiet for a moment, then said, "I go to church sometimes. I've seen you in chapel."

"I don't remember seeing you there."

"Yeah, well, I only go when I'm sure Smit won't see me, and then I sit way at the back. You know how Smit is about religion." He gave Drew a questioning look. "Does it bother you when he rags you about that?"

"Only bothers me he doesn't understand it," Drew said, shrugging. "I don't care about myself, but I feel bad for Jesus, you know?"

"What do you mean?"

"Well, I just think that if someone went through all that for everybody like he did, and it gets shrugged off—I dunno. That's gotta be hard to take." He put extra effort into wiping down the gun. "People don't stop to think that he's a person, too."

"You're nuts." Peterson snorted good-naturedly.

Drew laughed. "You're not the first person to think so! Hey, let me know if you ever want to talk about it more."

"No," Peterson answered. "It's not something I'm interested in. I'm just making conversation."

Drew nodded. "Okay. Well, I'm here if you ever want to. You know where I live. How about that wog roast, huh?"

Peterson blew the air out of his cheeks. "Man, if I never hear the Navy hymn again, it'll be too soon! I sang it a hundred times forward before I could sing it backward! I'm still trying to rub the grease off my face, too!"

"Listen," Drew said. "I just want you to know that I understand what's going on with you guys. You've gone through a lot together. But you need to know, Jack's not a bad guy."

Rising from his crouch near the gun's base, Peterson peered down at him. "I know. I think he's kinda cool. I hear he was some kinda dancer or acrobat or something. But Smitty doesn't like him."

"I get it," Drew said. "I hope it ends pretty soon before somebody gets hurt or in trouble." He nudged Peterson's arm. "I think you and I hit it off pretty good. Maybe we'll be the ones to help end it."

Peterson looked doubtful. "You don't know Smitty."

Chapter Seven

Dear Jack, Loretta's letter began.

Jack sat on the edge of his rack, oblivious to the noise of his shipmates as they tore into packages from home.

Jack heard none of it. The letter he was handed transported him back to New York. Reading Loretta's words, Jack could see her as clearly as though she were standing in front of him, an auburn-haired beauty with a figure that defined an enlisted man's dream.

Dear Jack, he read again. *You've been gone much too long, my dear. To make it worse, I know you won't get this letter for several weeks. I think it's about time you win this ridiculous war and get back home to us. Both Russell and I miss you very much. I'm enclosing a picture he drew of you.*

Jack withdrew another piece of paper from the envelope. Rusty had drawn him in a white crackerjack uniform with bucket hat. Cartoon Jack stood wide-legged with hands on hips. Almost every part of the tunic was covered with dozens of yellow crayon medals.

"How am I gonna live up to that?" Jack whooped. He replaced the drawing in the envelope and returned to Loretta's letter.

A lot has happened since I wrote you last. For one thing, I met Drew's girlfriend, Dorrie.

Jack grinned and looked around for his pal, but he was nowhere in sight. He continued reading.

She's a cute little thing, but unrefined. I'd guess she's about nineteen or so. Her accent sounds like Brooklyn, but not quite. I can't quite pin it down. One of these days, if I ever find a spare moment, maybe I'll take her aside for some makeup and fashion advice. I'd like to help her out.

She told me your friend plans to be a minister, and then she showed me his picture. My first thought was, what in the world can Jack and this boy possibly have in common? Drew really does look like her perfect match. He's young and adorable, with obviously no clue how the real world works.

"Huh!" Jack exclaimed, surprised and bothered by her comment. Maybe Loretta didn't understand what they were doing out here. Everyone was young, and Drew was hardly naïve. Anyone who could handle a cannon with the skill Drew did knew all about how the real world worked.

Write back quickly, Loretta's letter continued, *because I'm dying to know!*

P.S. I'm sending you an envelope by separate post with a copy of Marquee Quarterly. I'm on the cover! I'm finally getting out from under Moe Truett's shadow. I can't wait to hear what you think about it. It's creating quite a stir, and I'm sure it's going to open up a whole new world for me. I may even land a movie part if my manager plays his cards right.

Jack nodded, glad to read about her success. It was a well-deserved finger in the eye to the louse she'd married.

They told me at the Post Office that the package might not make it to you at the same time as this letter. Write and let me know what you think when you get it. I love you! We both send you hugs and kisses. Russell says to hurry home and don't forget to bring the medals!

Goodbye for now. Love, Loretta.

Jack looked around again for Drew. The Kid was sitting on the edge of his own rack now.

Jack decided not to bother him. He was reading a multi-page letter. If the moony look on the Kid's face was any indication, Jack was willing to bet the missive he was reading wasn't from his Aunt Mildred in Yonkers.

He sighed and re-read Loretta's letter. It would be a long time before he saw her again if the war dragged on. He was pretty sure that would qualify him for any insane asylum in the world.

"What's wrong, pal?" Drew's voice at his side said. "You look upset. Did Loretta send bad news?"

Startled, Jack looked over at Drew, who was parking himself beside him on the rack.

"Huh? Oh, no. Everything's fine. Get a load of this." He held up Rusty's drawing.

"Wow," Drew exclaimed. "Do you think he gave you enough medals?"

"I guess I should win at least one before I go home, huh?" Jack grinned. "Either that or dig into a box of Cracker Jack."

"Anything else happening at home?"

"Yeah. Loretta made the cover of *Marquee Quarterly*."

"What do you mean?"

"She's on the front cover. She's a model. Didn't I ever tell you that?"

Drew jumped up from the rack. "No! Hey, that's amazing! How could you forget to tell me something like that? You mean, she's famous?"

"Well, she's getting there. Won't be long now."

"Aren't you excited?"

"You bet!" Jack said. "But I knew it would happen. She's not only the best-looking dame on the planet, she's a showbiz brat. She did vaudeville when she was a kid, like I did. How about you, Kid?"

Drew's expression went soft. "Aw, Jack, I'm the luckiest man alive. Dorrie's the most amazing girl in the world. I've never known anybody like her. I still don't know why she agreed to marry me. Here, she sent a picture."

Drew handed Jack the black and white photo of his fiancée and watched for a reaction.

Jack played along, thrusting out his lower lip and mugging his approval at the girl's picture, although she wasn't much to look at, he thought.

As Loretta had said in her letter, Dorrie looked to be about nineteen. It was difficult to tell from the black and white whether she was a dark blonde or a light brunette. Nose too sharp, face too long. She wasn't ugly, but she was only a step or two away from being homely.

Jack didn't know what Drew saw in her, but his friend was head over heels. Jack didn't want to hurt his feelings. "Pretty classy, Kid," he said, handing the picture back to him.

Drew tucked the photograph back into the envelope. "She's something, all right."

"So, what's she say? What's happening back home?"

"Oh, well," Drew hedged, "She doesn't say anything as exciting as Loretta. Mostly personal stuff—you know."

Jack gave him a sideways grin. "Aw, mush."

"Like you don't know about mush."

"Like I'm the world champion of mush."

Drew's face brightened. "Hey, I almost forgot! Dorrie says she went to Loretta's house."

"Loretta mentioned that. She says Dorrie's cute."

"She's beautiful."

Jack was about to make a comment about life, romance, and women in general when a wild whoop at the other end of the cabin caught everyone's attention.

"Will you look at that!" someone yelped.

Everyone was gathered around a teenage sailor who held priceless gifts from home, the latest editions of movie magazines.

Jack and Drew exchanged glances.

"You think one of them is Loretta's?" Drew asked.

"Let's just wander over and take a look at what the Kid's got, just to be friendly-like," Jack suggested.

"The new starlets in Hollywood," the Kid with the magazines burbled excitedly.

Someone grabbed the magazine and whistled low. "Look at the dame on the cover! Did you ever see anything like that?"

Jack snatched it away from him. "Let me have that."

There on the cover, in full glossy color, was Loretta, posed on a fake sandy beach in a green one-piece bathing suit.

Drew slid Jack a look of awe.

Jack glanced up and around at his shipmates, then he froze, his gaze solid, his mouth tightening into a thin line of anger.

Drew followed Jack's stare.

Smitty was planting a kiss on Loretta's bright red magazine cover lips. With a sigh, he stooped and taped it on his rack locker drawer.

"Jack," Drew cautioned urgently.

The guys all laughed, taking Jack's pop-eyed response as the official Brian Jackson vote of approval.

Jack's fingers turned white with pressure as he crumpled the edges of the magazine.

"Hey, watch it!" the owner of the rag protested. "That's mine!"

Jack threw the magazine to the deck and took two rapid steps toward Smitty.

Drew lunged and grasped his arm, jerking him to a stop.

"Get off me!" Jack snarled. "He's gonna get what he deserves this time!"

Smitty looked up, surprised to realize Jack was talking about him.

Drew yanked him back another step. "Smitty's got a picture on his locker," he said *sotto voce*. "You've got the real deal waiting at home for you, and she's got a kid who thinks you're aces."

Jack's livid expression implied he was in no mood to be pacified, but he didn't make any further moves toward Smitty.

The crew watched in puzzled anticipation. Something was brewing, but what and why?

Unger and Peterson moved up beside their pal when they realized Jack was ready to fight.

"Get a grip," Drew urged his pal earnestly. "Do this and you'll wind up in the brig for decking this guy, and then you'll be up on charges in front of the Captain's Mast. What'll Rusty and Loretta think of you then? Instead of going home with a medal for the Kid, you'll have a record. Use your head."

Jack didn't take his glare off Smitty, but his heavy breathing began to slow and then stabilize. After half a minute, he took a deep breath and nodded at Drew.

Drew released his arm.

Jack visibly shook himself, then he snatched the copy of *Marquee Quarterly* off the deck and held it up. "The so-called *dame* you're all googly-eyed over on this cover just happens to be the woman I'm going to marry!"

There was laughter all around.

"Yeah, you and a million other guys," Peterson hooted.

Fearing another bout of Jack's anger, Drew yelped, "It's true! He's gonna marry her in real life! Her name's Loretta Truett and—"

Jack slid him an irritated glance.

Drew held up a hand and stepped back a pace.

Jack held the magazine up again. "I don't care if you believe it or not. This girl is going to be my wife as soon as this lousy war is over, and if any one of you puts this cover on their locker or even puts it under their pillow, they'll be getting a fist in the mouth from me. That's a promise."

Smitty stared at the photo, then back at Jack. "You're lyin'! There's no way you're gonna marry this broad, Jackson! Nobody ever gets married to a dame that looks this good."

"Brig, brig, brig," Drew hissed.

Jack ignored him. "Do you want to be the first one to find out?" he challenged Smitty. "Take the picture of my girl off your locker."

Smitty stood motionless, confused and uncertain.

Unger, standing beside Smitty, reached down and ripped the taped photo from the drawer. Holding it up for Jack to see, he tore the photo into four pieces and let them flutter to the floor.

"Hey—" Smitty said, but he let any other protests die. He glanced down at the ripped photo, then back up at Jack.

"She's got a ring to prove it," Jack said evenly.

No one believed it, but they let it pass. Let Jackson have his fantasy.

Drew walked back to his rack and pulled Dorrie's picture from the envelope. "Nobody holds a candle to you, honey."

***

Later that afternoon, after regular duty, Drew went to the Chapel to lay out the notes and Bibles for the study.

No one was there. Chaplain Mitchell was attending to business elsewhere on the ship. Because he was absent, Drew had orders to lead the study. Chaplain Mitchell had made it known that Drew was an official part of the ministry team, but so far, his shipmates were still unwilling to be taught by one of their own.

He gave up hope after half an hour. He sat on the bench in front, as usual and closed his eyes to pray, but looked up when he heard footsteps.

Peterson was standing near the door. "Hey, Brackman," he said.

"Hey," Drew answered.

Peterson coughed self-consciously. "Thought I'd find you here. What you did today, pulling Jackson back—brother, that was cool."

Drew shrugged and stood. "Didn't want to see him land in the brig."

"I was ready for a fight."

Drew grinned. "Didn't want to see you land in the brig, either!"

Peterson laughed. He pointed at the papers on the bench. "What you got there?"

"Bible study," Drew said. "I'm supposed to teach when Chaplain's not here, but no one ever shows up."

"Well," Peterson said. "I'm here."

"Swell, you want to do it, then?"

Peterson shrugged. He sat on the bench. "Sure, why not? I'm sick of checkers, and I don't have anything else to do."

"Okay." Drew retrieved a Bible and a set of notes and handed them to Peterson. "This lesson's from the Sermon on the Mount. Have you ever heard about that?"

"Sounds familiar," Peterson said. "My mom used to read the Bible out loud when I was a kid."

"Great, then maybe you'll recognize some of it. This is about something called The Beatitudes. Here, I'll find the chapter for you."

Chapter Eight

"That's it for the day."

The *Gilded Glamour Magazine* director for Loretta's new photo shoot extended a hand to help her to her feet. Her gold sequined evening gown fit snugly, making it difficult for her to balance unaided, especially on the smooth satin sheet she was posed on.

The sheet shifted as her stiletto heels slipped on the fabric. She'd have fallen if the manager hadn't caught her.

"Thank you!" She tugged at the tight fabric of the dress. "What sane person would wear a horrible thing like this in real life? It's a straitjacket!"

The director chuckled without looking up from his clipboard. "I guess that means you won't want to keep this one for your personal wardrobe."

"Only if it means I can have the satisfaction of putting it down the incinerator," Loretta exclaimed. "What torture!"

"Well, it looks good anyway, and so do you. That's what counts." He turned to address the photographers and crew. "Good work, everyone. We'll pick up again in the morning. You've all earned a relaxing night off."

The exhausted crew made sounds of relief as they picked up their equipment and supplies, more than ready to leave.

Loretta snatched her robe from the back of a wooden folding chair.

"Loretta," a voice from across the room said.

She turned to see her manager, Les Holt, a conventional-looking man in his fifties with hair as limited as his stature, come through the studio door.

Les was an acquaintance from her childhood. He'd managed her parents' transition from vaudeville to the legitimate stage, or at least tried to. A freak rail accident killed them before the contract was finalized.

When she needed a manager for her modeling career, she remembered Les.

She was glad she had. He'd handled her successful photo sales so far, even though until *Marquee Quarterly*, they'd been little more than glorified ads.

"What are you doing here, Les?" she asked as he approached. "I was just about to change out of this boa constrictor."

He nodded approvingly. "Looks good on you. Your *Marquee Quarterly* cover's already got serious buzz. If that's what you're wearing for the *Gilded Glamour* cover, we'll have a movie deal in a month."

She looked hopeful. "Do you really think so?"

"Sure, I do. My wife told me so last night! I always listen to my wife."

Loretta laughed. "Seriously, Les."

"I'm working on it. Moe's not happy that you're getting covers. He says you're violating the grounds of your divorce settlement."

Loretta snorted. "All the divorce settlement said was that I couldn't act for six years on stage. I'm not acting, I'm modeling. Besides, the six years have just passed. Do you want to know how I know?"

"Because you have a calendar?"

"No, because my son just turned six."

Les nodded. "The kid, right." He frowned, annoyed. "We'd be better off without that situation."

Loretta bristled.

Les held up a hand before she could respond. "I just mean the public doesn't like their idols to have pasts. I'm thinking practically. That's what you hired me to do, so don't bite. I think I might have an angle that will work well for us. Get changed and we'll talk about it."

Loretta gave him a curious look. "What is it?"

"First, change." He shooed her off with a gesture. "Go on."

She raised a curious eyebrow, then shuffled towards the dressing room as quickly as the dress would allow. A few minutes later, she reappeared in comfortable slacks, a sweater, and flats.

"Better," Les quipped. "The girl next door. You know, we should negotiate to get you a few casual covers, too. Then, every woman on the planet will think they can look as good as you do in that dress you just had on."

She pulled a chair closer, turned it around, and sat with her arms resting on its curved metal top, manicured fingers gripping the frame. "What's your idea?"

"How would you feel about doing a USO show? The publicity would be priceless."

Loretta shook her head. "No, sorry. You, of all people, should know I don't work for free."

"What about your sailor out in the Pacific?"

"What about him?"

"I got a call from the USO Executive Committee this morning. They found out that your boyfriend is out there. They asked if you'd like to go out with a show to surprise him."

Loretta shot to her feet. "See Jack? You mean on his ship? When?"

"In a few weeks. It's not only good for you and him, but it's good for business. This will put your career into high drive." He gave her a knowing look. "The war is very popular, and everybody's got someone out there. It will make them identify with you. What do you say?"

She chewed her bottom lip thoughtfully. "How long will we be gone? I have to think about Russell."

"We'll arrange for a sitter."

"He has a nanny," Loretta said, then a new thought occurred to her. "Although I have a new friend who might be willing to..." She wrinkled her nose, dismissing the idea. "No, I want Russell to grow up knowing better people than I did when I was a kid." Her eyes lit with sudden inspiration. "Although, hey. Did the USO say I could bring someone with me?"

"Who? Another entertainer?"

Loretta laughed. "No, a waitress from Kress."

"Come on, Loretta."

"I'm serious. She's a waitress from Kress."

"Oh," Les said. "No."

"Why not?"

"USO said it's entertainers only. They said they can't be responsible in case something happens out there. Not even family can go. Too dangerous."

"What do you mean, *dangerous*?"

"There *is* a war going on, you know."

"*How* dangerous?" Loretta repeated, more firmly.

Les sighed with exasperation. "The USO has done a lot of shows in combat areas. They know how to take care of their people. Can I guarantee it's safe? Of course not. Can I tell you it's probably safe? Yes."

Loretta pondered a moment, then said, "Let's do it."

***

Loretta had the cab driver drop her in front of the Kress Five and Dime at 5th Avenue and 39th Street, where Dorrie worked.

She wore an old cotton headscarf to hide her recognizable auburn hair. A large pair of dark sunglasses concealed her eyes. An old skirt, a sloppy sweater, and flats completed her disguise. Even she didn't recognize herself in a mirror.

The sudden celebrity generated by the *Marquee Quarterly* cover was fun, but her purpose this afternoon required her to remain anonymous.

"Wait for me," she instructed the driver. "I'll pay extra."

She entered the five-and-dime and walked towards the lunch counter at the back.

The store smelled of freshly oiled floors, old wooden shelves, leather, and wool. Wartime rationing diminished the inventory in the glass display cases lining the aisles, but there was still plenty of nice cheap jewelry, inexpensive clothing, and hard goods.

This place is just like an old friend, Loretta thought. Despite there being less merchandise on the shelves and in cases, it had changed little from her childhood. When her parents' vaudeville show had been booked in New York, they'd taken all their meals here.

The savory smells at the food counter weren't as rich and diverse as she remembered. The irresistible scents of bacon, coffee, and sausage that had once lingered in the air like culinary perfume were absent. Even the sound of sizzle on the grill was less active.

The menu board over the grill area offered things like spam and eggs (one egg per customer), grilled cheese, and vegetable soup.

Loretta braced one foot on the brass foot bar at the counter and jumped to sit on a high swivel stool.

Dorrie was taking a customer's order. Wisps of blonde hair escaped her cap and clung to her forehead.

"Excuse me, Miss," Loretta said, waving to get her attention.

"Hang on," Dorrie said without looking up from her pad. "Someone will wait on ya in just a second." She absently motioned for another waitress nearby. "Take that lady's order, will ya, Maggie?"

"No, no," Loretta said. "I want *you* to wait on me."

Dorrie looked up, annoyed.

Loretta lowered her sunglasses just long enough for Dorrie to recognize her.

Dorrie's mouth formed a soundless *Oh!*

She tore the most recent order out of her book and stuck it on the revolving metal cook's wheel on the back counter. "I'm taking a break, Billy!" she yelled.

"You just had a break!"

"I'm taking another one!"

"You want to keep your job?"

"Maybe, maybe not!"

There was no further response from the back.

Dorrie took two quick steps to Loretta, pushing the loose hair back under her cap. "What are ya doin' here!"

"Trying to get on the payroll, maybe," Loretta grinned. "Sounds like there might be an opening soon!"

Dorrie laughed. "No foolin', Loretta. What're ya *doin'* here? I saw your magazine cover! It's gorgeous! Everybody's talkin' about it. They don't believe I know ya, though." She shrugged. "Why should they?"

"Maybe I'll just let them know before I leave," Loretta suggested.

Dorrie's eyes lit. "Would ya do that?"

"Maybe."

Dorrie laughed. "That'll show 'em. I never thought I'd see ya again!"

"Why not?"

"Well, we don't exactly run in the same circles."

"Oh, tosh. I'm a vaudeville brat, like I told you. But listen, I'm here for a reason. Is there somewhere we can talk privately for a few minutes?"

"Sure," Dorrie said. "Follow me."

She came out through a half door cut into the counter and motioned for Loretta to follow.

Dorrie led them outside, just around the corner from the store. "It should be quiet out here. Everybody's already had their lunch breaks, and most people come into the store from the front."

Loretta nodded. "Listen, I have good news and bad news."

Dorrie looked alarmed. "The guys are all right, aren't they?"

"As far as I know, they're fine," Loretta said.

She told Dorrie about the USO tour, then explained that, though she'd tried, she couldn't arrange for Dorrie to come along.

Dorrie's eyes still shone with excitement. "It's okay. I mean, it's not okay that I can't go, but it's great that you can!"

"We take off in about two weeks," Loretta said. "I was wondering if there's anything you'd like me to give Drew?"

"A letter, for one thing!" Dorrie exclaimed. She clapped with excitement. "It takes four or five weeks for the guys out there to get mail from the post office. This way, he'll get it in just a few days!"

Loretta nodded. "Okay. Anything else?"

"Can ya give me a day or two to think about it? Maybe his mom and sisters might like to send somethin', too."

"Well, I can't take too much," Loretta cautioned. "I've already been told to pack light."

"Okay, we'll keep it small," Dorrie agreed. She hugged herself tightly, eyes glittering with excitement. "I can't believe it! I just can't believe it! You're gonna see Drew!"

Loretta grinned and nodded.

"Oh, and Jack, too, 'natch! That goes without sayin'! Ya must be so excited!"

"I am," Loretta replied, "but I'm nervous, too. We're going into a war zone, you know."

"I *know*," Dorrie breathed. "You're so brave!"

Loretta brushed it off with a wave of her hand. "Anything for our sailors at sea, you know!"

"Do Jack and Drew know yet?"

"My manager says that the Navy is keeping it under wraps as a surprise for the men."

"So, ya mean you're just gonna show up there, unannounced, like, and Jack's gonna have to deal with that right on the spot?"

"I guess," Loretta mused. "Maybe I'll ask them if they'd let Jack know a little bit ahead. Now, why don't I let your co-workers know that Dorrie Martin really does know the girl on the magazine cover?"

"Oh, thanks!" Dorrie said breathlessly. "This is gonna be so much fun!" She darted back inside.

Loretta gave her a few minutes, then walked in and to the back counter. She sat on the same stool she'd occupied a few minutes earlier. She slapped her hand on the counter. "Excuse me, can I get some service here?"

"Wait your turn, please," one of the waitresses snapped. "There's more than just you here."

"Well," Loretta said with mock indignation. "Unless my friend, Dorrie, waits on me, I don't think I want to eat here at all."

Dorrie sauntered over casually. "Well, what can I get for ya—" she looked over her shoulder at the wait staff—"my good friend from the cover of *Marquee Quarterly*, Miss Loretta Truett?"

Heads snapped up, but it wasn't until Loretta removed the sunglasses and pulled off the scarf, allowing her hair to tumble, that there was a significant reaction.

"This is my personal good friend, Loretta Truett," Dorrie said proudly, extending a hand.

Everyone descended then—wait staff, store shoppers, and diners alike.

Dorrie was shoved aside as Loretta was mobbed by people pulling out pens, *Marquee Quarterly* magazines, and any scrap of paper they could find to get autographs.

Loretta laughed brightly, basking in the glory of her first real professional fan mob.

When she'd finally had enough, she stood and extended her arms in a wide radius to keep her public at bay. "I really *must* be going now," she drawled, grinning and waving at Dorrie as she left.

Loretta's admirers followed her through the store and out the door.

Dorrie grinned and waved goodbye.

Maggie, the waitress, gaped at Dorrie, slack-jawed. She pulled an order book from her front apron pocket and extended it to Dorrie. "Can I have your autograph?"

CHAPTER NINE

"Battle stations! Battle stations! All hands to battle stations!"

At the call to general quarters, Jack was out of his rack and dressed shortly after his eyes opened. In seconds, he was scrambling with the rest of the gunners for the ladder and hatch.

The double *bong* of general quarters and the persistent demand to stations over the intercom spurred the men to a well-ordered and systematic stampede.

As they ran, they pulled on gloves, helmets, and yanked down sleeves until they were dressed according to regulation in case of explosion or fire.

There was no hint of nerves or fear. There was no place or time for them. Any man inclined to panic in battle had been weeded out in earlier action until all that remained was a crew of experts who knew their jobs.

A blast of hot night air assaulted Jack as he reached the last rung on the ladder, yanked open the hatch, and ran for the lower level and his gun.

Feet pounded on the decks as the pilots, gunners, and loading crews scrambled for position. On the flight deck, plane engines screamed like birds of prey. The steady *bong, bong* call to duty seemed to replace the sound of Jack's hammering heart.

Already drenched in night sweat and the spray from the sea, he hopped into his gun tub.

A shell burst over Jack's head and wailed into the night, throwing open a white parachute with a magnesium flare.

It was a drill, but Jack had no less of an adrenaline rush than if the call had been the real thing.

With unerring accuracy, he fired at the parachute, ripping it to tatters with the first explosion from his gun. He swiveled to sight the second, then the third, and the fourth, all of them within seconds of release from one another, his aim hitting the nearly impossible targets each time.

From his position and others around and beside him, the explosive ratting sound of machine gun fire destroyed each flare, even though the sky was black and visibility was almost non-existent.

Hellcat fighters roared off the flight deck to meet the imaginary foe, as eager to battle white parachutes and magnesium flares as they would have been to engage the enemy.

The skin on the back of Jack's neck tightened as the first wave of planes screamed overhead. Even though it was a game of war, his mind anticipated the spatter of strafing fire from Japanese Zeros.

If this were real, Jack thought, *I could be wiped out before I could take another breath. I'd never get back to Loretta.* It wasn't the first time in a fight or drill that the thought occurred to him, but this time it distracted him enough to miss the next parachute.

Smitty's gun, hammering next to his, took it out.

The pilots dove and zoomed overhead in an aerial ballet, distracting Jack from his momentary attack of anxiety and leaving him no time for another.

Soon, the sun rose over the horizon, and the mock battle ended.

"All clear!" the deck officer announced. "Gunners to the flight deck for observation and debriefing, on the double."

Jack whipped off his helmet and climbed out of the tub. He was first on the ladder to the above decks and had just mopped his sweat-drenched face with a sleeve when he heard an unearthly roar directly overhead.

There was a wild cry of warning. Someone bulldozed him hard from behind, knocking him down, face-first on the deck.

For a few long seconds, the pressure of a body on top of his didn't lift, then the weight shifted, and someone grabbed him by the arm and flipped him onto his back.

Jack dragged in a ragged breath. Blood coursed freely down his face.

"You okay, Jack? You okay?" Drew demanded, hovering over him, his expression urgent.

"Emergency unit!" someone yelled close beside him. "This man needs a stretcher!"

The sound of sirens and pandemonium screamed all around Jack, but still stunned, he didn't know what had happened.

He felt himself being lifted onto a stretcher. "What're you doing!" he demanded of the corpsman. "Get off me! I don't need this!"

The corpsman ignored him.

Jack looked up at Drew, still hovering. "What did you knock me down for, Brackman? What happened?"

Someone strapped Jack down.

"Get off me!" He demanded again, and again they ignored him.

"I didn't knock you down," Drew gasped. "It was—"

Unger's face lurched into Jack's field of vision as the medics lifted the stretcher. "Whattaya mean, what happened!" He pointed at something further down deck. "Didn't ya *see* it? Didn't ya *feel* it? Didn't ya *hear* it?"

Drew pointed in the direction Unger indicated. "Deck officer called all clear too soon! The *Hellcat* that was still coming in impacted."

"Full crash!" Unger yelled.

They lifted Jack's stretcher, and Unger and Drew ran alongside, ignoring the emergency crew's warning to disengage and return to their posts.

"It came in too low!" Unger yelled. "Smit just made sure your head stayed on your neck!"

The corpsmen gave the two gunners another warning, then rushed Jack away.

Drew and Unger stood huffing as they looked again at the carnage near the stern.

The plane's propeller had sheared off on impact. One wing was in tatters. Fire teams worked preemptively with foam and hoses to extinguish any fires that might erupt. Emergency crews crawled around the plane like ants on a carcass.

Unger wiped his forearm across his forehead, then exhaled and looked at Drew. "Smit just saved Jackson's life—on purpose! What're the odds of that?"

Drew did what he always did in any situation, good or bad. He thanked God.

***

Jack had a fractured nose but was otherwise unscathed. He was released within a few minutes and went in search of his savior.

Either they had ordered Smitty to another station during the emergency, or, as Jack suspected, Smitty was avoiding the man he'd saved.

The crash was the talk of the afternoon, and every time someone retold it, usually with gestures and sound effects, Jack realized how close he'd come to death.

The pilot hadn't made it.

Without Smitty's intervention, there might have been a second cadaver in the morgue.

Finally, at chow, Jack saw him at the end of one of the long tables in the usual company of Unger and Peterson.

Rumor was already rampant that Smitty was up for decoration for saving Jack's life. Jack couldn't think of a guy in the world who deserved it more. To save Jack, Smitty had put himself between the blade and the chopping block.

Jack grabbed a tray and wandered down to the end of the table toward him.

"Uh," he said, stopping behind his nemesis. "Um. Uh, Smitty, I don't know how to say this, but—"

"Then don't," Smitty grunted. "Just take a hike."

Unger looked up at Jack with a wry expression. "He says you're welcome."

Jack continued to stand at Smitty's place for a second or two, then, realizing he wasn't going to get another response out of the big man, he shrugged and turned back to his place.

"Hey!" Smitty called after him.

Jack stopped and looked back.

"I didn't save your life 'cause I planned to. I saved it 'cause the Navy trained me to have reflexes I can't do nothin' about. If I had my way, you and your head would be applyin' for separate addresses."

Jack winced, then stared, not understanding, and not wanting to understand, the kind of hatred Smitty had for him.

He returned to his place beside his friends.

"Don't worry about it, Jack," Drew said. "He's just embarrassed 'cause he did something nice. He doesn't want to make it obvious-like."

"Yeah," another shipmate confirmed. "Underneath that rotten exterior, he's just one big flowery valentine."

Jack laughed, then winced and put a hand to his face.

"Serves you right, breaking your nose," the same sailor quipped, spearing a Brussels sprout.

***

For several hours that night, Jack lay awake, unable to sleep. He faced the possibility of death every day, but there was something about the *Hellcat* almost decapitating him that spooked him like nothing else so far.

He hated questions without answers. Hated needing anything from anyone, especially someone like Drew, who always had that maddening calm about him.

When too many hours passed, he grumbled in annoyance and got out of bed.

Creeping to Drew's berth, he laid a hand on his shoulder.

Drew snorted, muttered something, and turned on his side, burying his face deeper into the slim pillow.

Jack grimaced. This was hard enough without the Kid complicating things. He glanced around to make sure he wasn't disturbing anyone else, not because he cared, but because he didn't want to get caught.

He jiggled Drew's shoulder, harder this time.

Drew gave one last snort, stirred, then opened his bleary eyes. The fuzzy vision of someone standing over him made him sit up quickly. "What the—!"

Jack planted a hand across his mouth. "Shut up. It's just me." He glanced anxiously around.

A few of the guys were stirring. One of them sat up to see what was going on, but then, too tired to care, dropped back on his rack.

Jack removed his hand from Drew's mouth. Straightening, he motioned for Drew to follow.

Drew came unsteadily, yawning and shaking his head with irritation. "Middle of the night, he wants to go for a walk," he muttered under his breath. "Can't wait 'til morning, no sir. Gotta get up right now."

Jack looked at him over his shoulder. "Keep it down."

Jack led them down a passageway near the berthing compartments, into the communal shower area.

The steel deck plating was cold under their feet. The sound of a lazily dripping showerhead echoed in the empty area and the relative quiet of the ship.

"Okay, what?" Drew demanded.

"Keep it down," Jack cautioned. There was little chance of anyone hearing them now, but he still kept his voice pitched low. "I want to ask you a question, but I'm warning you up front, if you preach at me, I'll cut you off, got it?"

Drew was still too sleepy to be polite. "*What* are you talking about?"

"I said, I want to ask you a—"

"I know, I heard you. Listen, Jack, you might not be able to sleep, but is that a good reason to wake a guy up in the middle of the night? I'd like to get back to bed, so make this good." He gave a huge yawn.

Jack raised an eyebrow. The Kid had been around him too long. He was beginning to sound like him.

"Okay, calm down." Jack opened his mouth, hesitated, then plunged ahead. "I was lying there awake, thinking about what happened on the flight deck this morning. I just thought I'd ask you what—" He hesitated, embarrassed. "What would have happened to me if I'd died?"

Drew shrugged. "I guess you'd be in the morgue."

"That's not what I mean." Jack held up a hand as though in defense. "Okay. What I want to ask is this. Where would—that is, where would my, uh—*soul* have gone if I hadn't made it out alive today?"

"Oh," Drew said.

Jack pointed. "No preaching, Brackman. Just the straight dope."

"Straight dope, without preaching."

"Right."

Drew hesitated. "Well, okay. After all the times you and I talked about—"

"What *you* believe in."

"What I believe in...well, did you ever—"

"Take the ticket?"

It took Drew a moment to realize that Jack was referring to the analogy he'd made several weeks earlier. "Oh, yeah, right."

Jack shook his head. "I don't believe in that stuff."

Drew's face screwed up with frustration. "Then why did you pull me out of bed to ask me?"

Jack waved his hand like he was batting an annoying fly. "Forget it! I'm sorry I asked."

He turned to walk back the way they'd come, but Drew caught his arm.

"You woke me up out of a good sleep and a nice dream, so you're gonna hear it. If you think I'm preaching, then okay. This is what I believe. If you die without taking God's way out, you get what you want. Not only that, if you take the ticket, you've got to mean it, not just say the words. It cost him a lot. You can't play games."

Jack smirked. "Or what? Wake up in your make-believe hell?"

"If that's the way you want it."

"What kind of answer is that? Who wants to go to hell?"

"Sounds like you do. Hell is just God giving us what we want. If we tell God we don't want anything to do with him, he'll back off and say, fine, have it your way. I gave you a break. If you don't want to take it—"

"Then it's not his fault if we miss the show."

Drew nodded. "Our fault, not his."

Jack was silent, gaze averted, then he glanced up. "You could be wrong, you know."

"I'm not."

"How do you know?"

"Because, God's Spirit's right here." Drew tapped his chest. "Inside."

Jack felt irrationally angry. "That's ridiculous! Do you know how crazy you sound?"

Drew shrugged. "You asked."

Disturbed and annoyed, Jack said, "I'm going back to bed."

Drew followed him out.

"I'll tell you what I believe," Jack said. "I think that when you die, you just snuff out like a candle."

"I guess you'll find out someday," Drew said.

As they rounded the corner of the passageway back towards the bunks, they didn't notice Smitty melt back into the shadows beside the showers where he'd been standing, listening.

Chapter Ten

The crew realized something unusual was happening when the *Yorker* detoured unexpectedly from its scheduled route.

The Captain had not announced a reason for the odd detour, which could have meant a few things. There'd been a false radar report earlier in the day that turned out to originate from friendly sources. The detour might just have been the Captain erring on the side of caution.

"Could be they're still tracking that ghost," Jack said. "Maybe we're going into enemy territory, and it's time to pray and pass the ammunition." He shrugged. "Or maybe it's shore leave of some kind. You gotta love the Navy, they always keep a guy guessing."

Jack's second guess was confirmed while he was busy helping the ordnance specialist, Mark Widdon, repair several guns that had taken shock damage from the *Hellcat* crash.

Yorker and several transport vessels were headed towards Echo Channel, near the main island of Azure Verde. The transport was a dead giveaway that civilians were on the way. The Island was a great spot for shore leave.

There was no sense of urgency, and the Captain had still not made an announcement.

"USO?" Jack wondered aloud.

Widdon, toiling with Jack on one of the guns, didn't stop working. He cursed with frustration as he vainly attempted to adjust the gun. Not only did the weapons need recalibration, but several had loosened.

"I don't want to see a USO show with you, Jackson. You'll just grouse through the whole thing about how the guys on stage are doing it wrong."

"You're right," Jack agreed. "Maybe I'll get up there and show them how it's done."

"I'd like to see that. Then maybe I can see if you've been lying all this time about how good you are."

He slammed the side of his hand against the cannon. "All Azure Verde means to me right now is that we'll be able to get help with this gun and a few of the others when we get there." He glanced down the length of the deck where several other men were working.

Widdon wiped perspiration from his forehead with the back of his sleeve. "That *Hellcat* did some real damage. They've got a good team of machinists stationed on the island. One thing's for sure: we can't leave 'em like this, and we need 'em fixed fast. We could use a few more experienced grease monkeys." He raised his gaze to scan the skies. "All quiet, but you never know."

"No one's ever attacked Azure," Jack said. "It's fortified. The enemy's not that stupid."

"Yeah, well Pearl was fortified, too," Widdon said. "Ask them how well that worked out."

Jack got to his feet. "Here's one gun that's ready for action. I don't think ten fleets of enemy gunners could make this thing come loose."

"That's stretching it," Widdon grinned. "We finally got the elevation and traverse adjustments right on this one. We'll have to give it a dry test soon. The civilians will love that. They'll either die from fright or they'll get a kick out of it." He slapped Jack on the shoulder. "Jackson, you're worth your weight in gold."

"Tell the paymaster." Jack mopped his face with his cap. "You know, maybe the whole reason we're detouring is to get help with the guns. That would make sense, wouldn't it?"

"Not with it all quiet and the transports headed in the same direction," Widdon nixed. "Nah, this is the Admiral's way of surprising his little swabbies."

He exhaled forcefully, exhausted in the heat. "Hopefully, this won't take long, and we can still see the show. We could all use a break." He looked pointedly at Jack's white-taped nose. "You've already had one break. You really think you need another one?"

"My quota's not filled up yet."

Widdon pointed at a transport vessel moving the USO troupe towards the Channel. "Look out there. See 'em? Any more doubts? John and Jane Citizen, on the decks of the transports. Is the Navy crazy? They're sitting ducks if anything happens."

"Nothing's gonna happen," Jack said. "Stop worrying. I'm sure the powers that be checked for safety after the ghost earlier."

Widdon gave him a skeptical look. "Now, you've really got me scared."

The intercom crackled, and the two men looked knowingly at one another.

"Here it comes," Widdon said.

"All hands, this is the Captain," the voice through the intercom announced. "By now, you're aware that we're docking at Echo Channel. A special USO show has been planned for this vessel. Landing craft will facilitate an orderly disembarkation."

Wild cheers erupted throughout the ship.

The Captain's voice continued. "The entertainment industry has always expressed appreciation for the work of our fighting men. Effective immediately, this crew, except those needed for critical duty, is being granted a twenty-four-hour leave to enjoy the special entertainment, which I'm told will begin in approximately an hour and a half, once the troupe has had time to set up."

"Critical duty," Jack scowled. "He talking about us?"

"Just us chickens," Widdon answered. "Let's see how fast we can get these suckers back up."

"The show will last two hours," The Captain's voice continued. "Afterward, leave will be granted. Remember who you are, men. I want an empty brig when you all return.

"Gunner's Mate Third Class, Brian Jackson, report to Captain's quarters immediately."

"Well," Jack said, "There's my official invitation to not go ashore." He kicked the base of the gun. "Thanks a lot."

"Don't kick that thing," Widdon joked. "It's dainty."

"Yeah," Jack groused. "Ain't we all."

***

"Gunner's Mate Third Class Brian Jackson reporting as ordered, sir." Jack came to attention and saluted as he entered the Captain's quarters.

Captain Fitzsimmons returned the salute. "At ease."

Jack gave the illusion of falling into a more relaxed military pose, legs shoulder-width apart, hands clasped behind his back.

Fitzsimmons sighed. "I have regrettable news, Jackson."

Jack nodded, already understanding. "I'm being kept aboard to help with the guns, sir?"

The Captain grimaced. "I'm afraid so."

"I understand, sir."

"There's more to it."

"Sir?"

"Stand easy, son. How shall I put this? I believe you know a young lady by the name of Loretta Truett."

"Yes, sir. She's my fiancée."

Fitzsimmons nodded. "Yes. She's also here with the show."

Jack stood frozen, incapable of responding for several seconds. "*Here*, sir?" He croaked. "You mean right now?"

"Here and now. She's on one of the transports to the island. From what I'm told, the ordnance and mechanics teams will need you on board to help until we can get assistance from Azure Verde. They're working on an assignment on the island that can't be interrupted. That may be well after the show is over."

Jack's throat tightened. "Sir, I haven't seen my fiancée for more than two years."

"I understand," Fitzsimmons said sympathetically, "but critical duty comes first, and there is nothing more critical than getting those guns back up."

Jack swallowed hard. "I understand, sir."

The Captain came forward and laid a hand on his shoulder. "You may miss the show, but there's still a twenty-four-hour shore leave. You and your fiancée will have time to be together. I'm very sorry, son."

Jack nodded tersely, eyes front and center. "I know you are, sir." A thought occurred to him. "Captain, I'd like to make a request. If Crewman Brackman is still aboard, I need to take a few minutes to give him something to hand my fiancée before the show."

The captain nodded. "The crew hasn't disembarked yet. You have my permission, but I need you back on the gun deck as soon as possible."

"I'll make it fast, sir."

Fitzsimmons saluted. "Dismissed."

Jack returned the salute and left. Once in the passageway, he choked back frustration and pushed the heels of his hands against his eyes, barely avoiding his taped nose, to regain control.

After a moment that seemed to last too long, he dropped his hands, opened his eyes wide, and took a deep breath. Then he went to find Drew.

Drew was still in the berthing compartment, so excited that he looked like the kid he was. When Jack explained the situation, his elation diminished. "Jack, I don't know what to say. I'm sorry."

Jack shrugged, trying to look cavalier. "It's only the show I'll miss. I'll see her after. But the idea of her being this close and not getting the chance to see her right away—" He hesitated as anger rose. He regained control and said, "I need to ask you a favor."

Drew nodded.

Jack went to his rack locker, rummaged in his sea bag, and withdrew a pencil and a pad of paper. He jotted a note, folded it, and handed it to Drew.

"Give this to Loretta," he said. "Tell her I know she's here and that I'll see her in a few hours. Tell her Jack said to break a leg."

Drew's eyebrows rose. "Huh?"

Jack's frustration surrendered momentarily to amusement. "It's a show business term. It means good luck."

"Oh." Drew pocketed the note. "Sure, I'll tell her." He gave him a sympathetic look. "It's only a few hours, Pal."

Jack nodded. "I know." He slapped his friend's shoulder. "Better ship out. They're starting to move."

Drew nodded again, gave his friend a thumbs up, and left to join the others.

Jack headed back to the gun deck.

Chapter Eleven

By the time the civilians and crew were ashore, Drew felt like he was back on the Coney Island Boardwalk in summer. There was no Ferris wheel, nor the smell of popcorn or cotton candy, but there was enough shoulder-to-shoulder humanity to make walking almost impossible, especially in the sand.

The crowd seemed more relaxed than when Drew had first arrived. An hour earlier, while he was still on the ship, there'd been some commotion. Distant aircraft were spotted on radar that turned out to be a returning patrol.

For a few minutes, some of the men had been called to their stations, but word came down quickly that it was a false alarm. Now, everyone was back to enjoying the show, though Drew noticed a few of the gun crew were still at their posts. Better safe than sorry, he supposed.

Drew gave up trying to reach the makeshift wooden stage up front. He thought about crawling on his hands and knees through the crowd, but he wasn't in the mood to be trampled.

He asked a stern-faced MA at the back of the crowd for help. "Hey," he said, approaching the man. "You're from the *Yorker*, aren't you?"

The tall man nodded.

"So am I. Can you help me out? You know Brian Jackson, the gunner from the ship, right? Well, see, his fiancée is Loretta Truett. She's one of the acts today.

"The Captain has Jack working on ordnance duty after the accident a few days ago." He realized he was babbling. "He can't get away for the show, and I have to give a note to his girl. Would you go up there and hand it to her for me, and—"

A microphone squealed from the front. "Is there a Drew Brackman in the crowd? Drew Brackman?"

Drew jumped. "That's me!" He looked at the MA. "Hey, they're calling me! That's me!" He jumped again, waving his arms to get someone's attention at the front. "I'm Drew Brackman!"

The MA grasped his arm and plowed with him through the crowd. Anyone prone to protest reconsidered when they saw the large security agent dragging a comrade-in-arms behind him like a pull-toy on a string.

As the man dragged Drew along, Drew saw Smitty, Peterson, and Unger.

"How'd you get so special all of a sudden?" Peterson yelled.

"Got to deliver a message to Jack's girl!"

When they reached the stage, the MA peered up at a man on the platform and said, "This is the man you're looking for."

The stage manager looked down at Drew. "You're Brackman?"

Drew nodded, wincing at a pulled calf muscle. He gave his burly escort a disgruntled look. "Yes, that's me."

The stage manager reached down and lifted the ropes high enough for Drew to duck and crawl under.

"Thanks," the manager said to the security agent.

The man gave a solitary nod. The sea of humanity parted again as he made his way back the way he'd come.

"You know Loretta Truett?" The manager asked Drew.

"I serve with her fiancé, Brian Jackson. He can't be here, and he asked me to deliver a note."

"She's been told," he said. "She asked me to find out if you were anywhere out there. Come on, she's in the tent in the back."

Drew followed behind, only beginning to realize he was about to be face-to-face with the most beautiful woman in the world. He felt a rush of panic.

"Everybody decent?" The manager asked as he ushered Drew inside. He didn't wait for an answer. "Better hurry, everybody, it's just about showtime."

Three women, hurriedly preparing for the show at makeshift makeup tables, crowded the small tent. They were all dressed smartly in Navy WAVE uniforms.

Drew recognized Loretta at once.

She sat at a small mirror, applying mascara.

The other girls had their hair piled in Gibson rolls, swept up, and tucked at the nape of their necks.

Unlike the others, Loretta's trademark auburn hair was loose. It swept across her shoulders and halfway down her back.

"Loretta," the manager said, "I found your sailor."

Loretta looked up from the mirror. Her eyes lit with instant recognition. "Drew!" She stood and rushed to him, throwing her arms around his neck. "Drew Brackman, I'd recognize you anywhere! You look just like your picture!"

She stood back as Drew tried to remember how to breathe.

"Uh," he stammered. "Thank you. So do you!"

Loretta pretended not to notice his anxiety. "They just told me that Jack can't make it to the show," she pouted. "I just don't understand that! I don't see why they can't make an exception. After all, we haven't seen one another for over two years!"

Drew nodded and pulled the note from his pocket. "This is from Jack. It might explain things."

She read the note and tsked with disappointment.

"Did he tell you he'll be here after the show?" Drew asked.

Loretta sighed. "Yes, but I wanted him to see it." She gave Drew a knowing look. "On the other hand, maybe it's best he doesn't. He'd volunteer to give everybody lessons, or worse yet, he'd take their places on stage."

The other two girls paused in their makeup applications and gave them curious looks.

Loretta hooked her arm through his. "Let's go outside for a few minutes. The show's about to start, but I need to talk to you in private."

She led him out of the back of the tent, where only a few stagehands and volunteers milled around.

Drew peeked around the side of the tent at the mass of naval humanity milling just beyond the ropes and the stage. He felt almost guilty for not being out there with them, but the feeling quickly passed.

"Dorrie and I have spoken a few times," Loretta said.

Drew's face lit up. "That's what she said in her letter! Is she okay? Does she look good? Did she say anything about me? Is she sorry she can't be here? Is she—"

"I don't have long," Loretta interrupted. "But I wanted to let you know that she gave me an envelope for you. I didn't want it to get lost, so I left it on the boat with my suitcase. I'll give it to you later."

Drew's happiness consumed his entire face, beginning with his eyes and extending through his wide grin. With Dorrie occupying his thoughts, he was no longer intimidated by Loretta.

The stage manager poked his head out of the tent flap. "You and the girls are on first, Loretta. Show time!"

Loretta squeezed Drew's hand. "Dorrie told me to say she loves you. Watch the show from inside the tent. We can talk more later."

"Thanks!" Drew exclaimed.

Loretta opened the show to good-natured cat calls, applause, and whistles from the crew.

"We're all so happy to be here," she said, looking beautiful but demure as she stood at the long-necked microphone. "Those of us from home can only guess what you brave fellas do for us out here." She smiled coyly. "But my fiancé, Brian Jackson, serves with some of you on the *New Yorker*. He writes me from time to time to tell me all about it."

A cheer went up from the *Yorker* crew.

Drew peered out of the tent, careful not to be seen. The *Valor Bay* trio had moved closer to the front. Even Smitty was whistling and clapping.

"Our friends, the Andrews Sisters, couldn't make this trip. They're touring with a Bob Hope entourage. But that won't stop us from giving you the best show you've ever seen! Let's get this ball rolling!" She looked over at the musicians stationed precariously close to the edge of the platform. "Hit it, fellas!"

The two other women in the tent brushed past Drew, jive-walking to join her on stage. Loretta took the traditional Patty Andrews lead while the other two provided backup harmony.

They performed "Here Comes The Navy," "Gimme Some Skin, My Friend," and "Don't Sit Under the Apple Tree."

When they finished, someone yelled out, "Boogie Woogie Bugle Boy!"

Loretta looked at her two companions. They exchanged glances, then grinned and nodded.

Loretta looked back at the crowd. "We haven't practiced that, but if you'd really like to hear it, we'll give it a try."

A roar went up from the crowd.

With a nod to the band, the trio launched into the popular song as effortlessly as though they'd practiced it as much as the others.

Loretta and the girls finished their set. After bows and blown kisses, they dashed breathlessly back into the wings.

"What I wouldn't give to have that kind of reaction back home!" one girl laughed.

Drew applauded vigorously. "You were great! You were amazing! You were all just great!"

Loretta grasped his hand. "Girls, this is Drew Brackman. He's a good friend of Jack's."

The two girls flanked him, kissed his cheeks, and ruffled his hair. "What's shakin', sailor?" one of them asked. "Doing anything after the show?"

"Writing a letter to his girlfriend back home," Loretta said pointedly. "Who happens to be a friend of mine."

One girl planted a kiss on Drew's cheek and withdrew. "I'm just fooling. You're a little young for me."

Drew pulled himself up to his full height. "I'll be twenty-one in two weeks."

"Really?" the second girl asked. "I wouldn't have guessed. No offense, but you look like a kid."

The following acts included a tap-dance quartet, a rendition of "Sing! Sing! Sing!" with an extended drum solo, a gymnastics team, and the comedy of The Victor Brothers.

Drew felt like he was home. All the horrors and stress of his last two years in the Navy melted away.

He and Loretta sat side-by-side in the tent, talking and laughing like old friends.

As the show wound down, Loretta said. "Excuse me, dear, it's time to close this one out."

"Aww," Drew complained.

She joined the other performers on stage to give final bows. "And now, we want to say thank you to every one of you by allowing you to come up and meet us. We'll also come out and mingle a little to give you a chance to get autographs."

The stage manager took the mike. "There's a lot of you out there. Please keep this safe and orderly. From what I understand, your security guys will make sure you do! If you're going to come up, do it single file. When the cast gets out there, be polite. God bless you guys! Glad you enjoyed the show!"

Loretta returned to the tent and snagged Drew's arm. "Want to be my personal bodyguard?"

"Glad to," he agreed. "There are a couple of guys I want you to meet out there."

Loretta extended her hand. "Lead the way, Admiral."

Drew took her hand as they stepped out into the audience. The surging audience separated them.

Several MAs restored order. Loretta pointed at Drew. "He's with me."

The security agents formed a protective wall behind and to the sides of Loretta and Drew. They moved through the excited throng as she signed autographs, planted a kiss or two on some lucky sailor's cheek, and shook hands.

Drew saw the *Valor Bay* trio moving up to meet her.

"These are the guys I want you to meet," Drew said. "They're on the gun crew with Jack and me." He reached out and grasped

Smitty's shoulder, pulling him forward, with Peterson and Unger not far behind.

"This is Bill Smith," Drew said. "We call him Smitty."

"How wonderful to meet you!" Loretta shook Smitty's hand first, then turned to the other two. "Any friends of Jack's are certainly friends of mine."

Smitty shook his head in wonder. "I thought it was a gag."

"What do you mean?" Loretta asked.

"Well," he stammered, "Jackson told me to take your pinup off my locker because he was gonna marry you. I thought he was kidding."

Loretta laughed with delight. "You have my pinup on your locker?" She reached out and cupped his rapidly reddening face in both hands. "You put it right back up there, sailor. That's where it belongs! I'll let Jack know I said it's okay." She gave him a friendly kiss on the cheek.

Smitty nodded like a smitten schoolboy, speechless for the first time since Drew had known him.

"And this is Tom Peterson and Carl Unger," Drew said, making the final introductions.

Loretta signed autographs for the trio, then, blowing a last kiss, she hooked her arm through Drew's. They continued to mingle.

Drew felt famous.

The *Valor Bay* trio trailed close behind, still stunned.

After a few minutes, an MA approached Loretta and Drew. "Ma'am," he said. "We've been asked to inform you that Gunner's Mate Jackson will join you here in about forty-five minutes." He inclined his head courteously and looked almost animated. "On behalf of the crew of the *USS New Yorker*, thank you for the show."

Drew leaned toward her. "Don't kiss him," he suggested in a whisper.

Loretta acknowledged the suggestion with a nod.

"Is it all right if I return to the boat to retrieve something?" Loretta asked the MA.

"To the transport vessel, Ma'am?"

Loretta nodded.

"We'll escort you."

"Come on, Drew," Loretta beckoned. "This is for you. I want you to come with me."

The microphone on stage crackled through the noise of the crowd.

"Hear this! This is not a drill," an urgent voice boomed over the sound system. "Repeat, this is not a drill! All hands to vessels for transport back to ship! Enemy fighters sighted, approaching this locale! USO troupes proceed immediately to designated safety areas. Crew nearest shoreline, report to command stations and transports on the double!"

Loretta looked at Drew in alarm. "What is he talking about?"

"Something that shouldn't be happening!" Drew gasped. He heard the sound before he saw the planes.

"Oh, my God!" Peterson cried.

Within seconds, they saw the dark shapes of the Japanese Zeros fast-moving toward the island.

"They're gonna strafe!" Unger yelled.

"Transport Three!" the MA barked, pointing toward a designated vessel. "Follow me, ma'am!" He started toward it, but the first strafing run cut between them and the water.

"Get her off the beach!" Smitty screamed. "Carry her if you have to!"

Loretta screamed in terror as the next flurry of fire tore up the sand between them and the transport, mowing down her escort and cutting off their route to the water.

The beach was in turmoil. Those permanently assigned to the island were already behind their guns.

A select dozen men, especially assigned to protect the civilians in case of just such an emergency, had already rounded them up and were bunkering them down to relative safety behind pre-built shelters and foxholes.

The next wave came seconds later, cutting down blue-shirted sailors in front of Loretta like wheat.

Drew saw the next attack coming. "Loretta!" He screamed. He launched himself at her as though he had wings.

"Brackman!" Smitty bellowed.

The Zeros passed overhead, their bullets peppering the beach, whipping up sand, blocking the girl and Drew from Smitty's view.

The planes looped back to regroup in the direction they'd come, screaming like victorious predators.

Before they could make another pass, Smitty reached Drew, whose body still shielded the girl. He threw him onto his back.

There was nothing left to identify the young man.

Loretta was unconscious, her dress smeared by Drew's death.

Smitty scooped her into his arms and spotted Transport Three, engines running. He sprinted across the sand, dodging bodies and debris. A sailor reached down and hauled them both aboard as the vessel pulled away from the bullet-chewed beach.

"Take her," he gasped to one of the crew. "Guns!"

"Above! Our best bet is to get to the *Yorker*!"

"Then get us there!"

Smitty sprinted for the deck, taking the ladder, three steps at a time. He dropped in place behind a .50-caliber machine gun.

Chapter Twelve

The *New Yorker* pilots and skeleton crew were already on deck, manning guns and scrambling into planes.

Chaplain Mitchell pounded down the deck, securing the strap of his helmet beneath his chin as he ran. He catapulted into the first empty tub and took up the gun.

"My girl's out there!" Jack bellowed at Widdon over the roar of approaching planes.

"Then let's stop 'em before they get to her!" Widdon yelled back.

The Zeros dive-bombed.

Widdon was hit and flew backward out of the tub.

Jack's gun released a burst of fire.

Bullets large enough to take his head from his shoulders screamed past his ears. He focused and fired again, the power of the guns reverberating through his bones.

His first score burst into flames and plummeted into the sea, nose first, like a dying bird.

Then somehow, Smitty was there, scrambling into Widdon's tub beside Jack. "Your girl's safe!" he thundered, his voice desperate and raw. "But Brackman bought it back there on the beach! He saved her!"

For several seconds, Jack didn't understand. Then his brain registered the words. Grief twisted his features. "You're a filthy liar!"

Smitty's face contorted. "I was there! I saw it!"

Jack clenched his teeth in a rictus grin of grief and tightened his hands around his weapon. He swiveled the gun, sighting the next wave of planes, firing whether or not the enemy was close enough.

Each mid-air explosion made him hungry for another. He poured his soul through the gun, the powerful emotions gripping him, replaced each time by exhilaration whenever another enemy plane burst into flames.

In his frenzy, he missed seeing the approaching Zero.

Smitty pivoted and fired. His aim hit, sending the plane into the ocean.

The enemy's final round ricocheted and tore into the gun base, sending shrapnel and splinters of steel whistling through the air. One heavy, jagged hunk struck the gun's mounting cradle. With a deep metallic groan, the massive barrel jerked on its pivot.

Jack was thrown hard onto the deck beneath it.

"She's loose!" Smitty bellowed. "Jackson, get outta the way!"

With a fatal groan, the cannon shifted again and came loose. The barrel fell onto Jack's legs, crushing him against the deck. Bones gave way with a sickening crack. He gasped. Then came the pain. He screamed as much from terror as agony.

He tried to move but couldn't. He felt heat brush his face as Smitty slid in beside him. Then somehow the pressure lifted, just enough. Hands grabbed him. Jack felt himself lifted into the big man's powerful arms.

"Corpsman!" Smitty bellowed. His arms threatened to betray him, already fatigued from carrying Loretta and shifting the gun to rescue Jack. "Corpsman!" He yelled again.

Glancing down at Jack's face, he could see the man was in shock. Gathering the last reserve of his strength, he staggered down the deck, trying to find help for his burden.

The deck of the *New Yorker* was in chaos. Men littered the deck like refuse. Flames roared on the stern from a downed enemy plane, despite the best attempts of the fire units to control it. Every corpsman was overwhelmed.

"This one needs help," Smitty gasped as he finally found a corpsman attending to a sobbing boy.

The corpsman glanced up only long enough to take stock of Jack's semi-conscious condition. He shook his head. "He's already in shock. Put him down there next to that one on the end, we'll get to him as fast as we can."

Smitty stared at him with disbelief. "He's bleedin' to death, you moron!"

"They're *all* bleeding to death!" The corpsman shouted. "Put him down and we'll get to him, I said!"

It was the last thing Jack heard for a time. He spiraled deep within himself to a place where there was no pain.

***

Jack drifted towards consciousness, his brain muddled by the steady drip of morphine. He marginally realized that someone was sitting beside his cot. It took him several seconds of concentration to recognize Smitty.

Smitty avoided looking at the other beds around Jack, all occupied by maimed and dying men. Kids, mostly. Some of them were far gone, most sedated, none alert.

Medics maneuvered around Smitty's chair, bothered by his presence, but too harried to argue with him to leave.

"I'm shippin' out," Smitty told Jack. "They said I could come down. Can you hear me?"

Jack concentrated, then nodded, his head gradually clearing. "Tongue feels thick," he slurred. "Where's 'Retta?"

"Safe," Smitty assured him. "Brought her aboard, myself. She didn't wake up for a while, but the medics said she's okay. They kept her in the Captain's cabin so she couldn't see what was out there on deck.

"I heard someone say the rest of the show people stayed on the island 'til the beach was cleaned up. They didn't see nothin', either. Civilians got the easy life. They got flown out this morning. Your girl left about three hours ago."

Jack groaned. "She's gone?"

"She wanted to come see ya, but believe me, pal. You wouldn't want her to see what's down here."

"You saved her?"

"Not me," Smitty said. He sniffed hard and wiped his sleeve under his nose in a nervous gesture. "The Kid saved her. All I did was get her to the ship."

"Drew—"

"Didn't make it," Smitty said. "I'm sorry to tell ya that. Unger and Peterson, and the Chaplain, too."

Jack closed his eyes.

"I just came by to say I'm sorry. I'm sorry about the Kid. I'm sorry about you. Like I said, I'm shippin' out. Word is they're sending me Stateside." He snorted. "I think they're scared I'll fall to pieces if I see another battle like *Valor Bay* or this one." He raised his eyebrows. "They might be right, too.

"There's just one more thing I want to say that I think you should know. Your little pal had guts. He wasn't big or noisy about it, like you and me."

He raised his eyebrows. "All that talkin' he did about God and stuff. Well, he had the ticket, so I think he's all right."

Jack couldn't answer.

"Okay." Smitty cleared his throat and stood, ready to leave. "Next time, you're on your own, pal." He saluted, turned, and was gone.

Chapter Thirteen

Dorrie's nightmares had always been the same. She would open the door, and sympathetic-looking men in Navy uniforms would be there.

She'd witnessed it happen to neighbors in her building—the shriek or wail that would compel her to open her apartment door to see what was wrong, and how she could help.

The Navy men always looked so handsome and regal in their full-dress uniforms. She couldn't help but admire them, even though she knew the tragic reason they were there.

It was Dorrie's habit to share lunch with Drew's mother, Katy, every day after work. Katy would open one or two well-worn photo albums, show her pictures of Drew as a baby, and fill her in on all the events, funny stories, and milestones in Drew's life.

When the knock came, Dorrie rose to answer the door. The first thing she noticed was the elegant, stiff-brimmed hats on the two men who stood there. She'd always loved the formal Navy uniforms. Something about that hat always grabbed her attention.

Was she dreaming again? Why would she focus so intently on a silly hat unless she was dreaming?

"Who is it, honey?" Katy called, then stood to join her at the door. She froze and stared at the men, just as Dorrie was doing. She cried out, "Don't tell me! Please, don't tell me!"

If one of the men hadn't caught her, Katy would have fallen. Firmly grasping her shoulders, he led her to an armchair.

Dorrie stared numbly at the other man who still stood at the door. "Come in," she said, her voice unnatural to her ears, as though someone else was speaking.

The man complied but remained close to the door. "My name is Lieutenant Commander Sullivan." He indicated the man comforting Katy. "This is Chaplain Gorman. Are you a member of the family?"

"I'm engaged to Drew Brackman," Dorrie said. She glanced at Katy. "The lady there is his mother."

Sullivan nodded. "Ma'am, I regret to inform you that Gunner's Mate Third Class, Andrew Brackman, died in action on February 26, 1943. The Navy offers its most sincere condolences and gratitude for his service and sacrifice."

Katy wailed and buried her face in the chaplain's shoulder.

Dorrie still felt artificially calm. "What happened?"

Sullivan gave her a summary of the battle.

"The USO show?" Dorrie asked, dazed.

"He knowingly sacrificed his life for another," Sullivan said.

Katy's sobs subsided, though she still clung to the chaplain's shoulders. She looked up as Sullivan walked to the chair and stooped in front of her. "Mrs. Brackman, I know how difficult this is, but we want you to know that your son died heroically to save the life of a civilian. It wasn't a mindless action."

"Civilian," Dorrie repeated.

Katy nodded mechanically at the chaplain, not really hearing, her face streaked with tears.

Dorrie's throat tightened. "What civilian?"

"Your son was Chaplain's Aide aboard his ship," the chaplain told Katy gently. "I know he was a man of faith."

Katy drew a sharp breath. "Drew loved Jesus!"

The first genuine wave of grief hit Dorrie. It crashed over her like a cold wave, but she held firm. She pressed her lips together and set her jaw. Katy needed her. Drew's sisters would need her soon, too.

"Thank you," Dorrie said, as the men headed toward the door. "Will they send Drew home?"

"Gunner's Mate Brackman's body is at rest in a Navy cemetery near Azure Verde Island. When the war is over, he'll be sent home with honors, ma'am."

He gave her a genuine look of sympathy and motioned for the chaplain to join him as they left.

Dorrie got through the rest of the afternoon in a fog of dull, throbbing grief not yet fully realized. It still seemed like a nightmare that would evaporate at any moment.

She held and prayed with Drew's devastated mother for an hour. At Katy's request, she called Drew's married sisters, Beth and Anna, and told them that they needed to come to their mother's home as soon as possible.

Something in her tone conveyed what words couldn't. Dorrie could tell from the long silences on the other end of the calls that the sisters somehow knew without being told. They didn't ask the reason for her call or the details. A few minutes later, they both arrived at Katy's house.

The family grieved, wept, and held one another. Though they included Dorrie in their grief, it was different for her. She wasn't a real member of the family. She hadn't known Drew his whole life.

Dorrie made a small lunch of sandwiches that no one ate. She sat and listened without speaking as they wept and shared stories about Drew.

At dusk, she kissed them all and took the train to her mother Agnes's house near Mount Vernon.

She told her mother mechanically what had happened. The dam burst, then. She fell into Agnes's arms, sobbing with the emotion that had waited for release.

Agnes held her and rocked her in her arms like a child. "You know Drew's safe with the Lord, baby," she soothed. "Don't cry. You know you'll see him again."

Dorrie knew, but in her grief, it didn't help. She knew he was fine, but she was not.

Agnes pulled back from the embrace. "You're not going home tonight." She wiped her daughter's tears with her hand. "You're going to stay here with me for the week. We'll get through this, and between the two of us, we'll figure out what comes next."

That night, after Dorrie was in bed and asleep, Agnes retrieved the evening paper from the front doorstep.

The bold, black letters of the headline told her whom Drew had saved.

Chapter Fourteen

Dorrie called in sick to work with no explanation.

"That girl's skating on thin ice if she thinks she can just take the day off without saying why," Edna, the manager of the Kress food counter, complained. "She'd better have a good explanation when she waltzes in here tomorrow, or she can kiss this job goodbye."

Dorrie's absence put a strain on the staff, especially the waitresses. Many of the women who'd served the counter had left to work in factories for the war effort. Some were finding new opportunities in offices and labor that the shortage of the City's men opened up. The new burden on the wait staff couldn't afford anyone to slack off.

The morning shift began. The brown tabletop radio sitting on the end of the lunch counter blared an early morning episode from gossip announcer Paul Campor's popular *Stay Tuned* radio broadcast.

America has a new sweetheart, ladies and gentlemen! Campor's famous rapid-fire report began. *Never before in the history of this country has there been such a sensational story of patriotism and sacrifice! Never again will we see this kind of heroic action, so incredible that it sounds like fiction!*

Edna snorted. "That guy needs to learn how to relax," she grinned as she grabbed a rag and wiped down the counter. "He talks so fast he makes me nervous." She slapped a hand on the ledge. "Come on, girls, wake up! I'm not gonna do everything myself. Somebody grab a rag and get the other side. The breakfast crowd will be coming any minute." She shook her head and muttered, "Thanks for nothing, Dorrie."

"Don't interrupt," one of the waitresses said. "I want to hear what's so incredible that it sounds like fiction." She hooted with derision. "Nobody can lay it on like Paul Campor."

"He's a card, for sure," someone else agreed.

Campor's breathless narrative continued. *This monumental story is true, and it happened just days ago in the turbulent South Pacific, where a war against the Japanese is raging! Add to that a USO show under fire, the sacrifice of a young sailor, a Navy gunner caught in the crosshairs, and his beautiful damsel in distress! Why, folks, I told you this story reads like a novel!*

The cook peeked over the top of the service shelf. "Hey, that magazine dame who was in here a few weeks ago to see Dorrie was doing a USO show. You think —"

"Nah," a waitress vetoed. "Stuff like that doesn't ever happen to people you really know. Shut up! I want to hear."

"Six a.m. is coming up fast, girls!" Edna warned. "Forget Paul Campor and help me get this counter ready, or it won't just be Dorrie whose job is in trouble."

"Just give it three seconds, already," the cook complained. "We'll get it done in time. Don't we always? I want to hear this."

Campor's voice continued. *Loretta Truett, the gorgeous Marquee Quarterly cover girl you've already come to ooh and ahh over, was squarely in the sights of Japanese gunners who invaded a USO show by air on Azure Verde in the South Pacific.*

A collective gasp went up, and the staff exchanged glances. "He *is* talking about her!" someone said. "It's that magazine girl Dorrie knows. No wonder Dorrie's not here today."

"Shut up," someone else snapped.

The entire troupe made it to safety," Campor's voice continued, *rushed to bunkers and other safe spots by our Navy cavaliers, but Loretta Truett was caught on the beach betwixt the bunkers behind and the transport ship ahead, unable to reach safety before the enemy began a deadly strafing run.*

Impossible! Death was all but certain for the ill-fated beauty until one of our brave boys sacrificed his life by shielding her with his own body. His name is being withheld out of courtesy to the family. Stay tuned until we learn more.

Silence descended like a curtain at the Kress lunch counter.

But it doesn't end there! Campor declared. *At the time of the attack, Loretta's husband-to-be, Brian Jackson, was a gunner aboard the Navy aircraft carrier New Yorker, anchored nearby.*

The New Yorker engaged the enemy, forcing the Japanese fleet to turn tail and run. But not before Brian Jackson was critically injured in the battle. The Navy has not given us specifics—stay tuned.

As of this broadcast, we know that Loretta Truett is still in the Pacific with her heroic gunner, who hovers between life and death.

How does this riveting story end? We won't know until Loretta Truett and Brian Jackson return home. Will Gunner's Mate Jackson survive? Will Loretta Truett continue her career, or sacrifice her livelihood to stay close by her gunner's side?

Only God knows. Until I learn more, I am Paul Campor with your Stay Tuned broadcast of the day.

Edna switched off the radio. No one moved or spoke.

Finally, Edna said, "Well, now we know."

"Poor Dorrie," someone else said. "You think Drew was out there?"

Customers began to trickle in and take their places at the counter.

Edna grabbed a handful of silverware and napkins to place on the counter. There was no more time to think about it.

Chapter Fifteen

Loretta was swallowed up in the white crackerjack Navy uniform the corpsman provided for her. She cinched it at the waist, but it still hung on her like a child dressed in adult clothing.

Her USO costume had been ruined, they explained. They hadn't wanted to go through her suitcase for a change of clothes.

She hadn't been allowed to see Jack in sickbay before they made her leave. He was to be transported to a medical ship for preliminary surgery before being shipped home. Upon his arrival in the States, she would receive notification of his hospital.

Despite knowing and caring, she felt calmly detached. She remembered the planes and the initial fright of the attack, but her recollections were like blurry watercolor images, recognizable but indistinct.

Exhausted, she slept through the long flight from New Caledonia, with a brief stopover in Fiji, before continuing to remote Canton Island, where a second refueling took place. Upon arrival in Honolulu, they provided her with accommodation on base.

"You'll still have nearly a full day of flying from Hawaii to California, and then on to New York," the pilot informed her. "It's best you rest on base overnight before continuing. Another flight will arrive tomorrow."

Her young escort, uniformed in dress whites, his features partially obscured by the rim of his hat, helped her off the plane and handled her bags as he led her toward her lodgings.

She got the first inkling of what waited at home as they neared the room.

The Honolulu Star Bulletin headline screamed at her in broad, black letters from the news box: *FASHION ICON LORETTA TRUETT BARELY SURVIVES JAPANESE RAID IN PACIFIC.* In smaller letters underneath was the subtitle: *USO Troupe OK.*

Loretta stared at the headline, stunned. She'd known there would be publicity around the incident, but she hadn't expected to be the focus, nor had she expected the news to reach the public so fast.

Her escort noticed the direction of her gaze. He reached into the news bin, removed the top paper, and turned it backward in the box.

"If it were only that easy," she said. "One good magazine cover and now I'm a fashion icon." She gave the escort a wistful look. "I wish you could follow me home to turn them all around."

A twin cot, wooden chair, dresser, and mirror comprised the room's simple furnishings. A small bathroom the size of a clothes closet housed a toilet and washbasin.

"Thank you," she said as her escort put her bags into the room. "Is there a place I can have dinner and make a phone call?"

"I can bring a sandwich to your room if you like, ma'am," he volunteered.

She smiled. "You're so thoughtful."

"Yes, ma'am. You also mentioned a phone call. I can make that for you, too, if you like."

Loretta nodded. "Yes, thank you." She sat on the edge of her bed, withdrew a fountain pen and piece of paper from her purse, and jotted a name and number.

She handed it to him. "This is my manager, Lester Holt. Please tell him to take my son, Russell, to his home or somewhere else that's safe. Let him know I'll call him when I land in New York, and that he should be ready to pick me up at the airport."

When he left, Loretta put her suitcase on the bed and unzipped it. On top was Dorrie's unopened envelope to Drew.

She stared at it. She had a fleeting mental flash of sitting in the tent with Drew, laughing and talking, then the memory vanished. Did Dorrie know yet? Were the headlines in the newspapers the same in New York?

She placed the envelope at the bottom of the case, refastened the bag, and lay on the bed with her head on the slim pillow.

She had nearly dozed off when there was a polite rap on the door.

"Come in," Loretta said, sitting up.

The escort entered with two sandwiches and a pot of hot water with tea bags dangling from the sides. "The canteen said they'll bring breakfast for you tomorrow. You won't need to go out there to get it."

Although she knew it was against protocol, Loretta stood and kissed his cheek. "I know I'm not supposed to do that, but I'm so grateful."

A blush rose in the young man's face. "That's all right, ma'am. There is one thing you could do for me, though."

"Anything," Loretta exclaimed.

He cleared his throat self-consciously. "May I have your autograph?"

***

By the time Loretta's flight stopped for refueling in Los Angeles and then landed at the Army's Mitchel Field in Garden City, New York, she'd been in the air for another full day.

A military escort assisted her off the plane with her bags.

"Is there a place I can make a phone call?" she asked.

"Yes, ma'am. Will you need transportation home?"

"Is that possible?" she asked, surprised.

"Yes, ma'am."

"Then, yes, thank you. I just have to make my call first."

He directed her to a bank of phone booths near the base exchange. Fishing a nickel from the bottom of her purse, she called Les's number.

He picked up the phone on the first ring. "Holt agency. This is Lester Holt speaking."

"Les, it's Loretta. I'm at—"

"Retta! Thank God! How are you? I got your message about Russell. He's here safe and sound at my place."

"I'm so sorry, Les. Does your wife mind?"

"She's happy to help. Right now, she's at the kitchen table helping him put a puzzle together. I'll be there to pick you up in a few minutes. Where are you?"

"The Army is giving me a ride. No need to come."

"The Army? I thought your guy was—"

"He is, but from what I hear, we all fight on the same side these days."

"Of course. How's Jack?"

"I don't know. A cannon fell on him. He's not great." She tsked, annoyed at herself for being sarcastic. "I'm exhausted, Les, you've got to forgive me."

"After what you've been through, I can't blame you."

"Is Russell okay?"

"Fine. He doesn't have a clue what's going on."

"Good."

"He's having fun. I have a dog and a large tropical fish aquarium, so between the two of them, he's content."

"Russell and contentment don't usually go together in the same sentence," she smirked. "How bad is it out there? The press, I mean."

"Press *and* fans. Depends on your point of view. Great, if you want publicity, lousy if you don't feel like being harassed after spending two days in the air."

"And nearly dying," she added. "Maybe I can get these nice escorts of mine to help me get into the house without being mobbed."

Les snorted with amazement. “It’s still hard to believe, isn’t it? A few days ago, we could only dream about this kind of publicity. I couldn’t have worked hard enough to make this happen.

“Don’t worry. There’s no one trying to get in the door here yet. When I picked up Russell at your place last night, they were just starting to gather. From what I hear on the radio, they’re at your place now, full force. Get here fast before they catch on that you’re here and not there.”

Only a few people were loitering around the fence of Les’s townhouse when Loretta arrived. Young girls, mostly holding copies of *Marquee Quarterly*.

One of them shrieked when she emerged from the car and ran toward her.

Loretta’s escort emerged from the car and positioned himself strategically between her and her fans.

Loretta ran up the steps with the escort behind her. Les opened the door before she could knock. He snatched her suitcase from the escort and pulled her inside. “Thanks a lot.” He gave the man a thumbs up and hastily closed the door.

“Was I supposed to give him a tip? They’ve seen you now. The rest will be here soon.”

Loretta fell into his embrace. “As long as they’re out there and I’m in here, I don’t care. You’re the best thing I’ve seen in what seems like forever.”

“Yeah, well, here comes the next best thing,” Les said, pulling back.

“Mommy, Mommy, Mommy!” Russell barreled down the long hallway from the back of the house with a golden retriever close on his heels. Behind him, Les’s wife, Betty, kept a polite distance.

Loretta knelt and opened her arms wide for the assault. She nearly went over backward as Russell catapulted into her arms.

“Hi, sweetheart, I’ve missed you!” Loretta laughed. She hugged him firmly. “Have you been a good boy?”

Russell pulled back and beamed up at her, his arms still around her neck. “Uh-huh! Have you been good, too?”

“Well, I’ve been as good as I could be!”

Loretta looked up as Betty approached. "How can I thank you?" she asked. "I know what a terrible inconvenience this is."

Betty shook her head. "Not at all. It's the least we can do." She put her hand on Russell's head. "He's a good boy."

Russell bounced up and down with excitement. "Did you see Uncle Jack?"

"Almost," Loretta hedged. "He said to give you one of these." She swatted his backside.

"Nuh-uh!" Russell protested. "Did you bring me the medal he's going to give me?"

Loretta hesitated. "I think he might have won a medal just a few days ago."

"Where is it!"

"They haven't given it to him yet. It takes a little while."

"Aw! I want to show it at school!"

Loretta stood, exchanging glances with Les and Betty.

"Remember," Les said, "he's six." He took his wife's hand. "Would you like to share a cup of tea with me in the kitchen, dear?"

Les looked over his shoulder and gave Loretta a thumbs up as they left, the dog at their heels.

Loretta sat on the sofa, pulling Russell up beside her. "Have you been having fun with Uncle Les and Aunt Betty?"

"Yeah! They got fish! Did you go on Uncle Jack's ship?"

"I did, for just a little while." Loretta measured her words. "Russell, while Mommy was visiting Uncle Jack—"

"With the SSO show!"

"That's right, with the USO show. Something happened, and Uncle Jack got hurt."

"Did he break his arm, like I did when I fell off the monkey bars?"

"Something like that, only a little bit worse. Uncle Jack is going to be in the hospital for a while."

"What made him get hurt? Was he in a big sea battle?"

Loretta huffed with surprise. "As a matter of fact, yes."

"Did he beat the bad guys?"

Loretta nodded. "Yes, he did."

Russell's face lit in a proud grin. "Yippee for Uncle Jack!" He pumped his small fist into the air. "I knew he'd do it!"

He jumped off the sofa. "I have to go tell Uncle Les and Aunt Betty!" Before she could pull him back, he ran down the hallway, shouting, "Whoo-hoo! Whoo-hoo! Uncle Les! Aunt Betty! Guess what? Uncle Jack beat the bad guys!"

Incredulous, Loretta sat staring at the far wall with her mouth ajar. "Well, that didn't go according to plan," she muttered.

Les poked his head around from the kitchen with a questioning look.

Loretta shrugged helplessly.

Chapter Sixteen

That night, with Russell in bed, Loretta nursed a glass of wine as she sat with Les and Betty in the dimly lit living room.

"The show was perfect," she said. "I met Jack's friend, Drew." She hesitated, not sure how to continue or even if she wanted to. The more time passed, the more she remembered.

"The sailor who saved your life," Betty prompted.

"Yes," Loretta said. "He was such a nice boy. We sat together at the show and talked for the longest time."

She hesitated. "He surprised me. He looked so young in that picture his girlfriend showed me." She took an absent-minded sip from the glass. "He looked the same in person, of course, but there was something about him I couldn't figure out." She mulled the puzzle over in her mind.

"No. I know what it was. He looked old for someone so young. That's the best way I can put it. It was like there was a man ten years older living behind those pretty blue eyes."

"War," Les said.

Betty nudged his arm. "You've never been to war, dear. How would you know?"

He frowned impatiently. "I don't need personal experience to understand what they're going through out there. I read the papers. I see the reports. It's got to be like waking up in hell every morning."

He shook his head. "I guess that's one reason the military takes 'em young. They go in thinking they're having an adventure. They come out like young, old men." He took a sip from his wineglass. "I can't imagine."

"Yes," Loretta said. "I'm sure that's what it is. And yet, he had the nicest laugh. It was like he'd been waiting for the chance to laugh and was glad to finally have one." She took another sip. "I liked him."

She shivered and hunched her shoulders as she remembered. "I saw the planes. There was a lot of noise, like thunder. I remember a sound like a buzz saw." She looked at them, her eyes asking if they understood and saw what she described.

"The men in front of me fell. It almost looked like they meant to, like it was some kind of Navy training or something. I thought that must be what it is." She focused on the memory. "I don't remember seeing any blood. Isn't that odd? There must have been blood.

"I just remember thinking, I've got to get to the boat, I've got to get to the boat. Then something hit me from behind, and that's all I remember." She hesitated, moistening her lips. "It was Drew. They said that I would have died if Drew hadn't pushed me down. Do you see?

"I don't know how to explain it, but it was like watching a movie. It was happening right in front of me, but it didn't seem real. It still doesn't. God help me if it ever does. That's all I remember until I woke up on a cot in Jack's ship.

"They wouldn't allow me on deck because of what I might see. They wouldn't allow me to visit Jack in the sickbay for the same reason." She shook her head. "The whole reason I went out there was to see Jack, and I never got the chance, even though we were so close."

"I should never have suggested that you go," Les apologized.

She tsked, returning to the present. "It's not your fault. I knew I was going into a war zone." She hesitated. "I just didn't understand what that meant."

Loretta lifted the glass to her lips. It was empty. She laid the glass aside.

"Want a refill?" Les asked, lifting the decanter on the end table beside his chair.

She shook her head. The alcohol made her feel mellow, and she didn't think she deserved to feel comfortable, given their discussion.

"How's Jack?" Betty asked.

"I'm not sure. They didn't give me details. They said they'll know more when I see him in the hospital. I know he's already had one surgery. He's due for another when he gets to the States, and God only knows how many more after that."

Les sighed and exchanged an uncertain glance with his wife.

Betty shook her head. "Not tonight, Les. You can tell her in the morning."

Loretta closed her eyes. "Please, Les. If it's bad news, I've had enough for a while."

"Not bad news," Les said. "Good news, but it can wait until morning."

She raised her eyebrows. "If you've got good news, give it to me now so that I can sleep tonight."

Les hesitated, then nodded, braced his hands on the arms of his chair, and stood. He walked to his Davenport desk in a corner of the room, opened the lid, and withdrew a large manila envelope.

He walked back, handed it to Loretta, then sat in his chair. "This came yesterday by special post."

"What is it?"

"Open it. It's an offer from Samuels Brothers Studios for a few scenes in the next Franklin Meadows film. Maybe two, if they like you."

"What!" She tore open the envelope and withdrew the documents.

"I've been negotiating with them ever since the *Marquee Quarterly* cover came out," Les said, "but they weren't convinced. Now, with what's happened, they're practically breaking down the door."

Loretta skimmed the pages of the offer. "Franklin Meadows!"

"Yeah," Les said. "He's a has-been from the last decade, but for now, he's still a draw."

Loretta looked up sharply. "You're calling Franklin Meadows a has-been?" She made a sound of amazement. "He's been my favorite actor since I was a little girl. I've idolized him forever."

Les shrugged and held his hands out, palms up. "To each their own. His acting is old-fashioned. He's still got some mileage, but not for long, I don't think.

"The studio knows you haven't done any screen acting. But given the attention you're getting from the *Marquee Quarterly* cover, and now this thing in the Pacific, they're willing to let him carry you through a few scenes, just to get your face up there and see how the public likes you. If it goes well, they might consider a contract."

She stared at the documents, still stunned, then shook her head and put them back into the envelope. "I don't have time for this right now. Jack needs me. I'll think about it in a few weeks."

"They're giving you ten days."

"How can they do that?" Loretta protested. "They know what's just happened. Jack isn't even back home yet."

"It's *because* they know what's just happened," Les said. He nodded toward the window. "If I go over there and pull back the curtain, how many faces do you think we'll see? You're getting free publicity right now. They're not even paying much attention to the other people who were there with the show.

"You're a symbol. You've even got fans. Every studio in the country wants a piece of that. Samuels Brothers is the first to make an offer, and they're the best."

Loretta looked confused. "I don't know what to do. The timing is wrong."

"Maybe Jack's not hurt as bad as you think," Betty said. "Besides, he might like that you've got this chance. He had his moment in the sun. He'll know it's your time now. I think he'll be glad for you."

"Listen," Les sighed. "You've got a little time. You don't even know what hospital Jack will be in yet. Betty and I want you to stay here, get some rest, and think things over. When they send you word about where Jack's going to be, I'll arrange for a car to take you to the hospital. Then you can talk to the doctor, talk to Jack, and make your decision."

Chapter Seventeen

Flying wounded patients back to the States from a war zone was not standard procedure, but Jack's injuries required measures the field surgeon was unwilling to attempt. A more fully equipped hospital might salvage his legs, but timing was critical.

Jack drifted in and out of consciousness, vaguely aware he was going home.

The medics worked quickly and efficiently. From the wreck of the *New Yorker*, they transferred him to a hospital ship. On board, he received surgical debridement to remove damaged tissue. Splints stabilized his legs, and a stiff board supported his injured back. Then they sent him to an air transport hub where he was prepped for the flight aboard a medically equipped C-54 Skymaster plane.

He felt ridiculous as he lay on a gurney in the hub, like a storefront dummy waiting to be stuck in a shop window.

"I'm giving you a sedative for the ride home," a nurse said, sliding a needle into his vein. "You don't need the morphine wearing off mid-flight before someone can give you another injection."

"How long before I'm back on my feet?" he asked.

"Well," she answered, "you're not ready to tap dance just yet."

"That's what I do."

She chuckled until she saw he was serious. "You're not joking?"

"I dance."

"Oh." She cleared her throat. "The sedative will make you feel relaxed, maybe even a little happy. You'll sleep most of the flight. Thirty-six hours or so, not counting refueling stops. The hospital Stateside will take it from there."

She left to attend to something beyond his field of vision.

He waited for the sedative to kick in. After a minute, he felt pleasantly tipsy. There had never been a war, he'd never been nearly crushed to death by his gun, and Drew was still alive.

The nurse reappeared to check on him. "They're just about ready to move you."

"Do you know," Jack slurred, "that you're a very pretty girl?"

"Well, thank you," she said. "You're not so bad yourself."

He fought to form words. "Have you ever been on the cover of—" he hesitated, then looked enlightened as he remembered—"*Marquee Quarterly* magazine?"

She snorted. "Not lately, but I've had my picture taken at Woolworth's. Does that count?"

Jack thought about it. "No."

She tsked. "Just my luck. Missed out on fame and fortune again."

He sighed, turned his head on the pillow, and was out.

The nurse shook her head. He was a looker, this one. She wished he hadn't mentioned he was a dancer. There was no way anyone could convince her that he'd even walk again, let alone dance.

She adjusted the blankets around him, made sure the straps were secure, and summoned an orderly.

"This sailor's ready to go home."

Chapter Eighteen

The Garden State Military Hospital, located in Newark, New Jersey, provided care for servicemen with major injuries.

The hospital gave Jack a private room. Normally, he'd have been given a bed on the ground floor with other patients. But even before he arrived, the press learned that Loretta Truett's war hero boyfriend would be there.

The press clogged the parking lots with reporters, photographers, cameras, and gossip columnists. They gave a blow-by-blow description, even if a teenage hospital volunteer emerged.

The hospital asked the police to take control of the situation. They did, but couldn't stop the public from coming and going. Newshounds still got in.

The press was waiting for her, despite police presence. She pushed past them, ignoring their questions and the flash of camera bulbs. She was given directions from the reception desk and took the elevator to the third floor.

She was allowed to sit outside Jack's room while he was processed and received treatment, but was not permitted into his room.

I get close, but I can never be with him! She fumed.

After an hour, a Red Cross volunteer brought her a sandwich and a cup of chicory. Later, she took a few moments to visit the ladies' room to freshen up and renew her makeup.

When she returned, a pretty middle-aged nurse with a kind face, dressed in a white military dress, found her. Her nametag identified her as *Donovan.*

"Oh, good," she smiled as she saw Loretta come down the hallway. "I thought you might have left."

"Not with those bloodsuckers out there," Loretta said. "Is Jack awake yet?"

"Probably not until tomorrow. He's spent a lot of time in the air, and he's been sedated much of the time. One of his surgeons would like to speak with you, though. Will you follow me?"

Loretta trailed her to the surgeon's office, unconsciously twisting the rings on her fingers.

Dr. Ronald Leesburg stood from behind his desk and greeted her with a smile and a firm handshake. He wore an olive-colored army uniform, covered by a drab smock. His face was pleasant, but uncompromising, as though he practiced the smile to soften the hard edges of his professionalism.

"Mrs. Truett, please come in. Sit down." He noticed her weariness. "I'd offer you a cup of coffee, but with rationing, the best I can offer is tea."

She rubbed the bridge of her nose with her fingertips. "It wouldn't do any good, but thank you, anyway."

Leesburg glanced down at his notes. "Gunner's Mate Jackson has no living family, I see."

"None," Loretta said.

"You'll be responsible, then, for any paperwork or consultations on his behalf?"

Loretta was surprised. "I hadn't thought about that, but yes, I suppose so."

"Very good. I've asked you here to give you the status of his condition and tell you what you can expect going forward."

"Please."

"He's not in pain. During this early stage of his treatment, we're carefully administering morphine. We alternate that with periodic nerve blocks and other pain management. Our supplies of morphine are severely limited. As he improves, we'll wean him off the drug. He'll experience discomfort, especially at first, but he'll adapt."

She pressed her lips and nodded.

Leesburg looked down at the clipboard in his hands. "Gunner's Mate Jackson sustained substantial injuries to both legs and the lumbar region. We will, of course, do everything possible to avoid amputation, but the damage to his limbs is severe."

Loretta shot to her feet, the color gone from her face. She opened her mouth, but couldn't speak.

"I'm sorry, but there's more you need to hear," Leesburg said. "He has fractured vertebrae in his lower back. Those bones support much of the body's weight. However, with time and therapy, his lower back will improve."

Loretta stared in disbelief. "Amputate."

Leesburg took her arm. "Why don't you sit down?"

Loretta mechanically obeyed. "You don't understand," she reasoned. "Jack and I are going to be married. We have plans."

"You can still be married."

"No one told me any of this. Why didn't someone tell me sooner?"

"A complete diagnosis was impossible until our surgeons could examine him more thoroughly. I believe this is what you were told, ma'am.

"Now, as for how he'll manage. Mrs. Truett, he's a young man in the prime of life. The chances are that he'll live as long as anyone. However, even if we save his legs, he may not walk again. It depends on how well he responds to treatment."

She sat stunned. "No," she stammered after a moment. "You must listen to me. You have to help him. Jack is a professional dancer."

"I'm sorry," Leesburg said. "He's scheduled for surgery in three days for vascular repair. We've already recommended his retirement from the Navy. I know this is a shock for you.

"There's something I want you to think about and discuss with him. Once he's recovered sufficiently here, he'll still require reconstruction therapy. The best option will be a facility located nearby. He'll receive excellent care."

Her jaw set. "I won't put Jack in a home."

Leesburg's eyebrows knitted with frustration. He massaged the bridge of his nose. "It's not a home, ma'am. It's a full-care Navy facility." He looked up with a tired sigh. "At least until his therapy is complete. The Navy will cover the cost of professional caregivers at a facility, but not at a private home on a full-time basis."

"I don't care about the cost. I'll find the money somehow. I'll hire a staff of doctors if I have to. I'll hire a whole hospital, but I'm not sending Jack away. I want him to come home. Does he know any of this?"

"Not yet. He hasn't been alert enough. We'll inform him when he's—"

"No," Loretta snapped.

Leesburg frowned. "Mrs. Truett, he has to know."

"Of course," Loretta answered, "but he'll accept it better from me. All I'm asking is that you give me a little time to find the right way, that's all."

Leesburg hesitated. "I'll respect your request if you can assure me that you'll tell him soon."

Loretta closed her eyes, relieved. "Thank you, yes. I'll be away for at least a week, but I'll leave contact information in case you need to reach me."

Leesburg frowned. "A week?"

"I have a little boy. I can't be here every moment. And isn't it better if I tell him after the surgery?"

Leesburg gave her a skeptical look.

"I promise I'll tell him when I come back. May I see him now, please?"

"You can sit with him, but he's not yet fully conscious." He walked to the door and opened it for her.

She remained seated. "Where can I make a phone call?"

"There's a pay phone in the lobby."

"I can't go out there. They're waiting to pounce on me."

Leesburg hesitated, then nodded. "You can use the phone here in my office. I'll wait outside."

***

"Holt Agency."

"Les, this is Loretta."

"How is he, honey?"

"It's bad. When I glanced through the documents from the studio, I saw what they're offering to pay. See if you can negotiate for that second role they mentioned, with the same salary. I'll take it."

"They mentioned that possibility, but right now, it's just a suggestion. You don't have a contract. I don't know if they'll—"

"Try, Les. I need the money. I want to bring Jack home, and it's going to be expensive."

"Isn't the Navy covering it?"

"Not if he comes home, and he's coming home. I'm staying at the Columbia Hotel here in Newark tonight. Can you please send a car to the hospital to pick me up?"

"Of course."

"Will you call the studio now?"

"As soon as I hang up."

"Thank you, Les. You're my angel."

"How are you holding up?"

"Lousy. Thanks for everything."

When she entered Jack's room, Nurse Donovan was checking his vital signs and jotting the results in a booklet.

The smell of antiseptic was pungent.

Jack's appearance shocked her. If she'd seen him by chance, she wouldn't have recognized him.

His eyes were closed. His complexion was sallow, cheeks sunken, mouth ajar. Pulleys and weights suspended both legs in traction. His broken nose was still taped from the *Hellcat* incident. Beside his bed on the opposite side, an IV bag pumped fluid into his left arm, which lay palm up at his side.

For an instant, looking at him, she saw the beach again. She felt the push from behind. She shuddered, waited for the memory to pass. It vanished as quickly as it had come.

She sat in the chair beside his bed and reached for his right hand.

She recalled the first time she'd seen him at a wrap party for some show. Looks attracted them both in the beginning, but it didn't take long for the superficial dross that initially drew them to burn away. Their bond had less to do with chemistry than mutual understanding.

They'd both grown up with vaudeville parents, they were both fighting for professional recognition, and they were both smitten with Russell.

Nurse Donovan noticed her hesitation. "He's not asleep," she said.

Loretta peered more closely at him. "He looks like he is."

"He's in Twilight. You can talk to him, but don't expect anything he says to make sense."

"Jack?" Loretta said tentatively.

His eyes opened slowly, his expression confused. "Dad?"

Donovan grinned at Loretta. "Told you. Have a nice talk. I'll be back in a few minutes."

Loretta squeezed his hand. "No, darling, it's Loretta."

He turned his head slightly, eyes narrowing as if trying to see through a fog. "I know you," he murmured with an uneven smile, proud of the recognition.

"You do? Who am I?"

"The girl at the party."

She nodded. "That's right."

"You're the prettiest girl in the room," he slurred. "I've known lots of girls. You're the best one."

She smiled, amused. "Do you know where you are?"

He thought carefully. "*Yorker.*"

"How would you feel if I told you that you're back in the United States?"

"On the ship."

"Home with me."

He considered for a moment, then gave her a puzzled look. "What happened to Drew?"

She felt doused with ice water. For a moment, she couldn't answer. Finally, she said. "Drew's in heaven."

"Oh," he said, surprised. "He must've turned in the ticket."

"What does that mean?"

"Ask *him*," he said sleepily. "He can tell you better than I can."

He sighed deeply, turned his head against the pillow, and closed his eyes. His breathing became rhythmic.

"Jack?" she prompted.

Nurse Donovan came back.

"Is he asleep now?" Loretta asked.

Donovan checked. "Out cold. It's nice you got to talk to him. He won't remember it tomorrow, but it'll give him peace of mind now."

"Thank you. May I ask a favor?"

"Of course, Ma'am."

"I have to leave first thing in the morning. If I write Jack a note, will you make sure he gets it?"

"Absolutely."

"Thank you." She withdrew a pen and a piece of paper from her purse.

Darling, She wrote. *I was here, and we had a nice little talk. I want so much to stay with you, but I must leave for a few days. My manager is taking care of Russell, and I can't leave him there for long. I'll be back as soon as I can, once I've made arrangements for him. At least we're not an ocean apart this time. Please hold me close to your heart - Love, Loretta.*

She handed the note to Donovan. "Thank you. I'm expecting my car to arrive. Until it comes, may I stay with him?"

"You take as much time as you want," Donovan assured her. "When he wakes up, I'll be sure to let him know you were right here, sitting with him."

Loretta nodded, grateful. "The staff here is very kind."

"Most of us have family fighting out there," Donovan answered. "When we help the men who are healing here, it helps us, too."

When she was alone again with Jack, Loretta touched his cheek. "What have they done to us, darling?"

"Mrs. Truett," Donovan said from the doorway.

She glanced up.

"They tell me your car is already here. He says he's been waiting. The front desk sent someone out to have the driver come to the laundry chute area in the back. That way, you don't have to go through the newspaper people out front."

"It doesn't matter," Loretta shrugged. "They'll just follow him to the back."

Donovan's right eyebrow quirked. "Not with our security team, they won't, ma'am. They saw what happened when you first got here."

Loretta's expression melted with gratitude. "Thank you. How wonderful you've all been."

"It's okay," Donovan said. She hesitated, then added. "If you don't mind me saying so, we were all amazed by your picture on the cover of *Marquee Quarterly*, but this new one made us wonder if you were really just a human being, like the rest of us."

Loretta was confused. "The new one?"

"The *Gilded Glamour* magazine cover. You look beautiful in that gown."

Loretta gasped with surprise. "I forgot about it."

Donovan bit her lower lip and shifted her weight. She looked uncertainly at Loretta, then gave a resigned sigh.

Loretta thought she knew what she wanted. "Did you want to ask for my autograph?"

Donovan wilted with relief. "I didn't want to ask, but I *really* wanted to ask!"

Loretta laughed softly. "Do you have the magazine with you?"

Donovan held up a finger. "Wait right here." She darted out into the hallway but was back almost immediately. "This was on my tray. Please don't let anyone know I asked. I could get in trouble."

Loretta accepted the *Gilded Glamour* magazine. "You didn't ask, I volunteered." She looked at Jack. "He'd be kidding me about this right now."

She glanced down at the cover and was jolted with surprise. She'd seen the proofs shortly after the shoot, but artistic enhancements and the magazine's glossy cover made her look ethereal.

"It turned out pretty good," she said as she signed her name and handed the magazine back to the nurse.

Loretta stood and leaned down to kiss Jack's cheek. "I'll be back soon," she whispered. As an afterthought, she added. "I'm very sorry about Drew."

A startling thought occurred to her. She still hadn't contacted Dorrie.

Chapter Nineteen

Les's call came as Loretta arrived at the hotel.

"We'll give you a few minutes to get settled, then we'll send the call on up," the man at the front desk said.

The phone in her room rang as she got inside.

Loretta kicked off her shoes, sat at the small writer's desk, and picked up the phone receiver. "You can put the call through now."

There was a moment of silence, a click, then she heard Les's voice.

"They're willing to meet your terms," he said.

Loretta exhaled with relief. "Two movies?"

"Two. Free publicity is worth a fortune to them, and that's what you'd be giving them. You'll only have minor roles until they see what you can do, but wow! What a payday. They added another five hundred to what they first agreed to give you. The owner of the studio, himself, wants to meet with you the day after tomorrow at two o'clock."

Loretta sat up straight. "Morris Samuels?"

"The one and only."

Her mouth twisted with frustration. "Les, I—listen, I left Jack a note telling him I'm going to New York to take care of Russell. He'll think I lied to him. I didn't expect all of this to happen so fast. They know it's only been a short time since the raid. How can they do this to us?"

"Relax. This one's just a meeting. Filming won't start for at least six weeks, but they want to get the publicity mills grinding. You'll have plenty of time to be with Jack and figure out what to do with Russell.

"The studio is sending a charter plane for us tomorrow at Newark Army Airfield. That's close to your hotel. The flight to L.A. will take fifteen hours, give or take, with a refueling stop along the way."

Loretta closed her eyes and rubbed her left temple with her fingertips. "I feel like I was born and raised in an airplane. Do me a favor. Call the hospital and give them the Studio's phone number. Ask them not to call me until after we meet with Samuels. You have the details, right?"

"Right."

"Jack's surgery is on the same day, and I need to know what happens." She felt pressure building behind her eyes. "If you hadn't given me that time to rest at your house, darling, I think I'd have gone crazy by now."

His next words were cautious yet concerned. "I can call them and say you've changed your mind, but I don't recommend it. This is the chance of a lifetime."

"No, I can't cancel," Loretta said. "I can't let this go. It's too important."

"You're not wrong. Listen, I know how hard this is—lousy timing. But you're being very smart, and not just because of this whole thing with Jack. Modeling is fine for the next few years, but you won't be twenty-four forever. You need something else to fall back on. I've been your manager and your friend for too many years not to care. I owe it to your folks to look out for you."

He hesitated, then said, "Have you seen the *Gilded Glamour* cover? It makes *Marquee Quarterly* look cheap. I'll see you tomorrow morning at ten o'clock. Be ready to go."

Loretta replaced the receiver on the hook but didn't remove her hand from it. The nightmare of the day wouldn't end until she made one more call.

For several minutes, she stared at the phone, picked it up, put the receiver back on the cradle, and picked it up again.

At last, she dialed Dorrie's phone number.

"Hello?" It was Dorrie's distinctive New York accent.

Loretta couldn't respond.

"Hello?" Dorrie's voice said again.

Loretta hung up the receiver.

Chapter Twenty

As he awakened from surgery, Jack felt as though someone had stuffed his head with gauze and wrapped his tongue with the leftover material.

"Water," he croaked as the first hint of consciousness drew him towards the surface.

Nurse Donovan approached his bedside with a paper cup full of ice chips. "Open your mouth," she ordered.

Jack cracked open one eye and gave her a suspicious look.

"Ice chips now, water later," she explained. "You've just come out of surgery. Come on, now, sailor, open up. This won't hurt a bit."

Reluctant and feeling silly, he complied.

She sprinkled a few slivers of ice from the cup onto his tongue.

Jack had never tasted anything as good. "Thanks," he croaked.

"How do you feel?"

He indicated the cup with a gesture, and she gave him a few more chips. "Am I supposed to feel this bad?" he asked, as the ice melted down his rough throat.

"Yep," Donovan said. "You might even feel worse a little later. You've been sedated for several days, and you're coming out of anesthesia after surgery."

"Thanks"—he coughed and winced—"for the reassurance."

She gave his arm a sympathetic pat. "Do you remember Mrs. Truett being here?"

His eyes brightened. "Loretta's here?"

"She had to leave, but she left you something." Donovan reached into her smock pocket and withdrew the note. "A very nice lady. As famous as she is, I'm surprised she was so friendly." She handed him the note.

Jack gave her a quizzical look. "Famous?" He wondered what he'd missed. Was her magazine cover doing that well? He unfolded the note, blinked to focus, then frowned.

Donovan raised her eyebrows at his disappointed expression. "Bad news?"

"Not her fault," Jack answered. He laid the note aside and indicated the cup of ice she still held. "Can I keep that?"

"Not yet. As dry as your throat is, you'll be tempted to gulp the whole thing."

His head continued to clear as the minutes passed. After fifteen minutes, he became more aware of the antiseptic smell of his room and the starkness of his surroundings. There were soft voices in the hallway just beyond his door, the occasional scuff of rubber-soled shoes on linoleum, and sometimes the sound of squeaky wheels on carts.

For the first time, her remark about surgery registered. "Where am I?"

"You're in the Garden State Medical Hospital."

"Garden State, like in New Jersey? You mean, I'm back?"

She nodded. "Yep. This place will be home for a little while."

Jack examined the small room with his gaze. Four white walls without pictures or decorations, except for a medical chart on the far wall. A white-tiled ceiling and white sheets and blankets. Beside his bed, there was a white metal table that held water in a white container, a clear glass, and a radio.

"If that radio wasn't brown, this place would disappear," he muttered.

"It's better than a ship crammed to the portholes with a thousand other guys, isn't it?"

"Flat-top doesn't have portholes."

"Well, you know what I mean." She put the cup of ice on her cart. "Your therapist will be in a little later today."

"For calisthenics?" he asked, amiably sarcastic.

She chuckled, caught off guard. "Not quite. We thought you might enjoy breathing exercises instead, just to give you a real challenge."

"What's wrong with me?" Jack asked. "I remember the cannon dropping. How bad is it?"

"That's something you'll have to discuss with your doctor."

"Is he coming in before or after I learn how to breathe?"

She laughed lightly. "My goodness, you're just naturally sarcastic, aren't you?"

He snorted and smiled. "It's a gift."

She pulled a chair up alongside his bed. "Mr. Jackson, we're going to be together for a while. I don't want you to think I'll ever take you lightly. You've gone through a lot, and you have a lot more coming.

"My husband is with the Army in Italy. I'd like to think that if anything happened to him, God forbid, someone would be kind to him. That's why I'm working here, and I really do care."

Jack hesitated. "Your husband's a lucky guy."

"I think so," she smiled.

Chapter Twenty-One

Loretta wasn't prepared for the chaos of Samuels Brothers Studios. As the limo carrying her and Les passed through the gate, the lot seemed like a world within a world, more fantastic than the one outside.

She stared like a star-struck teenager as the car wound through the myriad back lots. Boxy beige and gray soundstages, towering like cliff faces, loomed over the landscape. Tall metal markers beside each rectangular playhouse displayed the studio logo and the title of the movie in production. A light attached beside the ventilators, high on the wall, flashed red, indicating filming was in progress.

Ordinary-looking people in day-to-day street clothes scurried throughout the miniature city with armloads of colorful costumes and wigs. Some pushed carts of lighting and heavy film equipment. One young woman balanced herself on a bicycle as she steered with one hand and held a stack of scripts in the other.

Loretta recognized Tula Withers, a star famous for her elegant European accent and refined features. She wore a Louis the Fourteenth period costume and was smoking a cigarette as she walked across the lot, reading a script, mindless of where she was going.

Les pointed discreetly at her as their car passed. "The thermometer just hit ninety-five degrees. How much would you bet she'd kill to get out of that get-up right now?"

Loretta giggled and nudged him. "How much would you kill to be her manager?"

With the windows of the limo partially lowered, they could smell the mingled scents of fresh-cut lumber, cigarette smoke, hay, and dust that created their own unique perfume.

The car rounded the corner and parked in front of an office building that looked nothing like the soundstages or other buildings they'd just passed.

Loretta wrinkled her nose. Art Deco architecture, with its geometric patterns and silver, red, and black flourishes, made the building look as though someone had plopped it down amid the more modern structures when no one was looking.

Les noticed her expression. "I know Art Deco isn't your favorite style, dear, but this office belongs to Morris Samuels. Right now, you love it."

Loretta's eyes widened as she fully realized what they were doing. "Oh my gosh, Les," she hissed at him under her breath. "Are we really here?" She couldn't breathe. "I can't do this!"

"A little late to decide that," he said drily.

The driver came around and opened the back door for them. "Mr. Samuels's secretary is expecting you," he said.

He assisted Loretta out of the car and held the door for Les.

The same Art Deco style decorated Samuels's outer office. The young secretary in the reception area sat behind a desk that resembled three silver triangles intersecting under the rim of a black-and-white tile top. Floor-to-ceiling portraits of current stars lined the walls. Smaller pictures of movie stars from every era, including those from twenty years earlier before sound, surrounded the larger portraits.

Lying on the secretary's desk were copies of Loretta's *Marquee Quarterly* and *Gilded Glamour* magazines.

The secretary looked up and smiled as they ushered her and Les inside.

"Please have a seat. I'll let Mr. Samuels know you're here."

Loretta wondered if the sweat she felt on her face was noticeable and if her perfect makeup job was melting.

Les noticed her nervousness and patted her hand. "You survived death by inches not long ago. This is nothing compared to that."

She nodded and blew air out of her pursed lips.

A minute later, the master of the house, himself, emerged from his inner sanctum.

Loretta and Les stood to meet him.

Morris Samuels looked like a benevolent old grandfather. He wore a suit that, while tailored, still seemed too small for him. A glittering chain attached his gold watch to his vest. Round spectacles accentuated kind-looking eyes.

He extended a hand first to Loretta, then to Les.

"Mrs. Truett, I can't tell you how eager I have been for this meeting," he said warmly.

"Oh," she said, trying to keep her voice steady. "Thank you, sir. I've looked forward to it, too."

"After what you've recently gone through, please accept my apologies for having you come all this way from the East. If our shooting schedule wasn't so tight, I would have waited to bring you."

Les exchanged a glance with Loretta. "I thought shooting didn't start for six weeks," he said to Samuels. "That's what I was told on the phone by your representative."

Samuels looked confused, then abruptly enlightened. "Oh! Oh, no, sir. Mrs. Truett has been offered roles in two movies. It's the second one that begins shooting in six weeks."

"Oh!" Loretta exclaimed.

"Come into my office, both of you," Samuels said. He turned to his secretary. "Marcy, will you please bring in a pot of tea? Maybe a few pastries?"

Loretta wasn't surprised that Samuels's inner office was also decorated in Art Deco. She and Les seated themselves in chairs close to his desk. Copies of Loretta's magazines were also on the mogul's desktop.

"How is your fiancé, Mrs. Truett?" Samuels asked, settling himself in his leather swivel chair.

"Thank you for asking," Loretta said. "Jack's in the hospital, I'm afraid."

"So, I hear. My sources inform me he suffered injuries during the battle that nearly killed you."

"Yes, sir."

"But he's not the young man who saved your life, if I understand correctly."

"No, sir."

"Mm-hum," He said thoughtfully, glancing down at the two magazines. When he looked up again, his expression was less sympathetic. "And all this happened recently."

"Yes, sir."

"Remarkable. You're very brave to start a new profession after such a horrible personal ordeal. I'm sure it would take me a lifetime to recover from something that brutal."

"Sir," Les interjected, "I know the timing looks bad, but please remember, we're here at your invitation. I insisted Mrs. Truett come because I thought she wouldn't be needed for at least six more weeks."

Samuels grunted. "I see. So is she prepared to refuse our offer?" He raised his eyebrows. "Our agreement is for two films."

"No, sir," Loretta said. "To be honest, I need money to pay for Jack's medical bills."

Les shot her a look of alarm.

She stood, and Les stood with her. "I'm sorry if we misunderstood the terms, but I can't leave my fiancé for such a long time."

"You're her manager," Samuels said to Les. "Are you going to let her abandon this opportunity?"

Marcy's arrival with a silver-trimmed wagon holding a pot of tea, three cups, and several pastries, interrupted them.

"Just put it here beside my desk, Marcy," Samuels instructed.

She complied. "Is there anything else, sir?"

"This is fine for now, dear, thank you."

When she left, closing the door behind her, Samuels repeated his question to Les. "Are you counseling her to abandon this opportunity because she's unwilling to make both films?"

Loretta had never seen Les look nervous. He was sweating now. "Mr. Samuels, Mrs. Truett is my client, but she's also a longtime friend. I'll stand behind any decision she makes."

"Mm-hum," Samuels said. He stood and attended to the tea tray. "Sit down, both of you. How do you take your tea? Is two lumps of sugar sufficient?"

Samuels didn't wait for an answer. He took his time, carefully pouring three cups of tea. He used the tongs to add sugar and put the cups on saucers. He leaned across the tea server, handing a cup to each of them. "Pastry?" he asked. "It's from our commissary, so I promise it's very good."

"No, thank you, sir," Loretta answered.

Samuels returned to his desk. "Now, Mrs. Truett, I have a personal question for you, and it's impertinent, so I beg your pardon in advance. Please don't answer if you feel uncomfortable. I promise you there's method to my madness."

She gave a cautious nod.

"I've been in contact with the management of the USO troupe that was on the island during the attack. Only weeks ago, you were caught in the middle of a battle. A young man died defending you. Is that an accurate description?"

Loretta met his gaze without answering.

"It's all right," Samuels said. "I told you that you don't have to answer, but I'm asking because I need to know your state of mind. This studio is a business. I don't want to go to the expense of publicity or begin shooting if you're going to have a nervous breakdown in the middle of production.

"Your roles in these movies are small, but you've become a sensation with the public. Your modeling career was already getting quite a bit of attention. Now, after what's happened, you're being called America's new sweetheart. That is an asset to this establishment. We'd rather not let an opportunity like this pass.

"I need to know if you're going to cost this studio money and embarrassment if I hire you. I also need to know if you think you can handle the responsibility."

Loretta was silent. "Mr. Samuels," she said after a moment. "I remember most of what happened, but I can't promise I remember everything. All I can tell you is that it hasn't affected my actions so far. I don't believe it will. I don't know what else to tell you."

Samuels considered that. "Thank you." He glanced at Les. "Mr. Holt, are you listening?"

Les raised his head, his expression grim.

"Mrs. Truett," Samuels said, returning his attention to her. "I'm sympathetic to the reasons you've given for wanting these roles. I appreciate your honesty. Your situation is unimaginable to me. I'm sorry if you and your manager misunderstood our terms. I believe, though, it would be in both our interests to continue with our plans.

"Here is my proposition. Shooting on your first film with Franklin Meadows begins in a little less than two weeks. While your role is small, your presence will be required throughout filming in case of the need for reshoots. If it's possible—and only if it's possible—I'll have a charter plane fly you from the studio every month or so to visit your fiancé wherever he is. You'll spend a few days with him, then we'll fly you back to fulfill your commitments here. Is that acceptable?"

Les glanced at Loretta.

She nodded. "Yes, sir."

"Excellent." Samuels clapped his hands together once with satisfaction. He pressed a button on the intercom on his desk. "Marcy, will you please ask Bob Lowell to come in?"

"Right away, sir," Marcy's tinny voice responded over the machine.

"Bob is the head of our publicity department," Samuels explained. His eyes glinted with enthusiasm that hadn't been there moments before. "We need an angle that will put the public on your side, Mrs. Truett. If I had questions about your reasons for returning to work so quickly, the public will, too."

A moment later, there was a light rap on the door.

"Come in, Bob," Samuels called.

A young man dressed in khaki pants, canvas sneakers, and a short-sleeved white knit shirt entered.

Samuels indicated Loretta with a gesture. "Say hello to your next project, Bob. I'm sure you recognize her from her photographs."

Lowell grinned and extended his hand to Loretta. "Nice to meet you."

She shook it, then introduced Les. "This is my manager, Lester Holt."

Lowell shook his hand, too. "A pleasure."

"Now, Bob," Samuels said. "We have a problem, and we need you to fix it."

Samuels explained the situation.

"Well," Lowell said. "Her need to pay the medical bills is an angle that takes care of itself." He threw his hands out. "I don't see the problem. It makes her look great."

"It would humiliate Jack if he knew I was helping him," Loretta said.

"Well, we don't want that," Lowell said. He looked at Samuels questioningly. "Do we?"

Samuels shook his head. "Let's leave the boy some dignity. He was an up-and-coming entertainer on stage. He'd just completed a successful run in New York when he joined the Navy."

Loretta's mouth fell open with surprise. "How did you know?"

Samuels looked back at Lowell. "What else can you suggest?"

"Well," Lowell said. "We could say that he insisted she return to work to get her mind off what happened."

"No," Samuels said. "That makes her seem petty. What else?"

"How about using what happened at the USO show? We can say she's doing it for the boys. She also wants to honor that kid who saved her life. The studio could donate to the USO from whatever box office we take and tell them it's her contribution." He shrugged. "We can always write that off on the taxes, and it makes her look sympathetic. Mutually beneficial."

"Very good," Samuels approved. "Especially if we also add that she's flying back and forth every few weeks to visit her boyfriend in the hospital."

Loretta felt like a stranger in her own drama. "Excuse me. Do I have a say in any of this?"

"For the time being," Samuels allowed. "You're not under contract. Do you have something to add?"

"I do. The young man who saved my life comes from an ordinary background. I know his family is grieving. After what I've been through with the press over the last several weeks, I don't want them to suffer through that, too. Will you leave Drew Brackman and his family out of your plans?"

Samuels exchanged glances with Lowell. "We'll go with that angle. Leave the dead boy out of it. Release the story to that windbag, Paul Campor, and the other gossips, and let's get this show on the road." He grinned at his own unintentional pun. "So, to speak.

"Mrs. Truett—may I call you Loretta? Do you plan to leave this afternoon?"

"I have a child," Loretta said. "If I'm going to work at the studio for several weeks, I need to find a school for him and a place to stay."

"We'll handle that," Samuels said. "We have a plane waiting at the airport to take you home. Be with your fiancé for a few days. Rest up a little. We'll fly you back again on the weekend. Before you leave, I'd like you to meet Franklin Meadows. He's finishing up a film this afternoon, and I believe he's available."

Loretta's eyes widened. Meeting her childhood crush on the spur of the moment wasn't something she'd expected. "You mean now?"

"Unless you feel the need to return home right this minute."

She glanced at Les.

"Meet with him now," he advised. "One less thing to deal with later."

"That would be fine, then, Mr. Samuels," she said.

Samuels nodded. "Good. Bob, take them to sound stage Five, will you?"

"Sure thing."

As Lowell opened the door, Samuels called to Les. "Mr. Holt?"

Les turned at the door.

Samuels spread his hands. "Most of my negotiating was done with Mrs. Truett. Is there any reason in the world that she brought *you* along today?"

Chapter Twenty-Two

As they followed Lowell across the lot, Les pulled Loretta back so only she could hear.

Looking behind, Lowell realized they wanted privacy. "Meet me at Sound Stage Five," he said. "You can't miss it. It's just around that last corner. See it?"

Les nodded and waved. "Thanks. We'll be there in just a few seconds."

When Lowell was far enough ahead, Les said. "I let you down in there. I'm embarrassed, and I'm sorry."

Loretta hooked her arm through his. "You were there with me, and that's what I needed."

Les removed her arm from his. "I wasn't there as your friend this time. I'm your manager." He tsked, disgusted with himself. "I've never dealt with power brokering on this level before. This is the first time I've done business with anyone on a studio level. I was nervous."

"That makes two of us," Loretta said. "Don't worry, we'll get through this together." She stopped walking and gave him a weary look. "I think when we get home, I won't visit Jack right away. I've been on the go almost non-stop for weeks. I think I've logged more airtime than American Airlines. If I don't rest, it's going to catch up. I'll collapse and I won't be good to Jack or anyone else."

"I agree," Les approved. "Don't worry about Russell, either. He'll be fine with Betty and me until the studio finalizes your temporary living arrangements." He grinned and folded his arms, rocking back on his heels. "Okay, then! Are you ready to meet Franklin Meadows?"

She shook her head vigorously.

Les grinned. "Go on. I'll wait for you out here."

"Les, come with me!"

He grinned. "You're going to be working with him for weeks. You may as well get to know him." He gave her shoulder a playful nudge. "You'll be fine."

***

The inside of the soundstage was a jungle of wires, arc lights, and boom microphones on tall swivel poles. Operators positioned massive cameras on dollies high enough above the sets to capture the best shots and lighting. Cables snaked across the floor, connecting critical equipment to expensive sound recording and communications systems.

The make-believe worlds were there, too. In one corner, a modern office interior sat directly next to a medieval courtyard, complete with artificial landscaping and elaborate Gothic garden furniture. Another area housed a rocket ship with a pointy red nose on its launch pad, while a neighboring farmhouse was waiting for a horse or cowboy to appear.

The soundstage was cavernous but still crowded.

Loretta marveled at how so many sets could be crammed together in one indoor location.

Filming was not in progress, and actors and actresses in colorful costumes milled about, talking, smoking, and eating.

Lowell guided Loretta expertly through the maze. At the center of the mayhem, across the soundstage, she saw Franklin Meadows.

Meadows's face lit up when he recognized her. "Hello, there!" he boomed from across the soundstage. "They told me that my new starlet might come today!" His voice was distinctly British. "Wait right there. If I don't break my neck on these cables, I'll be right over."

As he approached, Loretta saw that he looked older in person. But with his warm brown eyes, pencil mustache, and square jaw, he was still the matinee idol of her dreams.

"Loretta, meet the star of the movie, Frank Meadows," Lowell said. "Frank, this is Loretta Truett. She'll be starting with you soon."

"I know full well who she is," Meadows said.

Loretta tried to remember she was an adult. She extended her hand. "I know who you are, too! It's nice to meet you, Mr. Meadows. I've enjoyed your work."

Meadows grinned. "Call me Frank. I've enjoyed yours, too. Someone just handed me a copy of *Gilded Glamour*. How did I get so lucky?"

Loretta laughed, surprised. "Do you actually read those things?"

"Lately," he said, "I've just been looking at the covers. Are you free for lunch? I've just finished a seven-week schedule, and I don't want to think about moviemaking for at least the next hour. I'm so famished, I could eat a small dinosaur." He reflected on his statement and lifted a quizzical eyebrow. "Is there such a thing as a small dinosaur?"

She laughed. "Thank you, I'd love to, but I can't stay long. I'm on my way to the airfield after this."

"Leaving so quickly?" he asked, surprised.

She nodded. "My work here doesn't begin right away. I have to go back home for a few days to be with my fiancé."

His expression became serious. "I read about what happened to you in the newspapers. And who hasn't heard the radio broadcasts? I'm very sorry. I've performed in several USO shows, but I think we're all rethinking that after your nightmare."

She was about to thank him when she heard her name.

"Is there a Loretta Truett on the lot?" someone called from across the chaotic arena. "Loretta Truett?"

She glanced up and saw a technician holding a phone receiver above his head.

"Oh, my gosh!" she gasped. "I forgot! Excuse me, Mr. Meadows. I've got to take this!"

"It's Frank!" he called after her.

She skirted across the cable-strewn floor and took the phone from the aide. "Thank you." She put the receiver to her ear. "This is Loretta Truett."

"Mrs. Truett, this is Doctor Leesburg."

Loretta forced herself not to hold her breath. "I was just about to call," she lied. "This is the first chance I've had to talk. How was Jack's surgery?"

"He came through it well. Aside from the obvious, he's young and healthy. Our team doesn't think that amputation will be necessary."

Loretta made a soft sound of relief.

"I don't want to give you false hope. He's still not out of danger, but we're optimistic."

Loretta sat on the edge of a nearby three-legged stool and put her face in her hands.

"Mrs. Truett?"

Loretta felt weak. "Yes, I'm here."

Meadows watched her from across the room. She was exquisite. It wasn't difficult for him to envision himself alone with her. He was rehearsing in his mind how to ask her if he might drive her to the airfield when he saw her put her face in her hands. She looked close to tears.

"As you and I discussed," Leesburg said, "You have to let him know. Even with this positive prognosis, he may not walk again. At this juncture, we still don't know."

She didn't answer.

"Would you prefer I do it?" Leesburg asked.

Loretta shook her head, as though he could see her.

"Mrs. Truett?"

"I'll tell him," she said. "I won't be there for at least three days, and I'll have to leave again a few days later."

"Three days is a long time. He's asking questions and doesn't understand why we're not giving him direct answers."

"He's awake, then?"

"He's alert."

"Will you let him know that I'll be there soon?" Another startling thought occurred to her. "Will you remove the radio from his room? Don't deliver any newspapers to him, and caution anyone taking care of him, not to mention anything they hear about me in the news."

It was Leesburg's turn to be silent.

"I have things to tell him," she explained. "It's better that he hears it from me and not from the press or through gossip."

"Unusual requests," Leesburg said, displeased. "But there doesn't seem to be much about your life that's ordinary. I'll inform the staff and his medical team, and I'll have the radio removed."

"Thank you so much, Doctor. I'm so sorry for the inconvenience. So very sorry."

As she hung up, Meadows approached cautiously. "I hope I'm not intruding. You look like you could use a listening ear right now." He smiled. "Or a glass of water?"

Loretta glanced up, too emotionally drained to be embarrassed. "No. No, thank you. I'm fine."

"You don't look fine. Not in the least."

"It's just that so much has happened in such a short time." She choked back tears.

Meadows led her to a folding chair in a corner, away from the noise and chaos of the soundstage. He let her weep. After a few seconds, he withdrew a handkerchief from his breast pocket and handed it to her.

"Thank you," she sniffled into the linen. "Just look at all of this around here." She made a sweeping gesture. "All of this magic is so exciting and fun that I forgot for a little while. It was almost like being alive again, instead of being trapped by people screaming questions at me and flashing camera bulbs." She stamped her foot. "And I'm sick to death of airplanes!"

"It's all right," he assured her. "Who were you speaking to on the phone to make you so upset?"

"Jack's doctor," she said.

He raised an eyebrow. "Is he dead?"

She gave a short, surprised laugh. "No, he's not dead. But when I tell him what's wrong with him, he'll wish he were." She sniffled again, then remembered who she was talking to.

"Oh, and this is the worst of all! I'm meeting the movie star I've loved since I was a kid, and I'm blubbering into his handkerchief!" She slammed her fist down on her leg. "This is the ending to a perfect month!"

Meadows chuckled and assisted her to her feet. "Your makeup is a mess."

"I know!" She wailed.

He took the handkerchief and dabbed at the smudges around her eyes. "Don't worry. You're still beautiful."

Meadows put a comforting arm around her shoulder. "Listen, I know that the roles they've given you in these first two movies are small, but they're going to lead to bigger things."

She sniffled and glanced up at him. "Do you think so?"

"Yes, especially if I have anything to say about it. Besides that, you'll be with me on screen. Come on. I'll walk you out." They made their way to the tall elephant doors, gathering curious and suspicious looks from the crew, actors, and staff.

"You may not believe me right now, Loretta, but I want to tell you something," Meadows said. "And I don't want you to think I'm being cavalier. I've had my share of troubles. Who hasn't? I promise you there's nothing like a good day of work to put things into perspective.

"When you get back here in a week, they'll work you so hard you'll forget your problems. This place is a sweatshop!" He laughed and waved his hand to assure her he was kidding.

She looked up at him through the last lingering tears.

"You'll see!" he assured her.

Chapter Twenty-Three

"Why are you taking the radio?" Jack demanded as the little brown box beside his bed was unplugged.

The middle-aged workman in faded overalls and a flat cap put the appliance under his arm and toted it towards the door. "Don't know," he muttered without looking at him. "I'm just the janitor. I do what I'm told."

"Well, bring it back!" Jack demanded. "It's the only thing in this igloo that has any color to it!"

The man cast him a disgruntled look but left without answering.

Jack let his head fall back against the pillow with a sound of exasperation. He was exhausted and sick of getting no answers from his doctor about his condition.

Boredom was becoming a way of life. He knew it was a problem when he looked forward to the cleaning lady coming in once a day to mop the floors and dust the already obnoxiously clean room.

Visits from his physical therapist didn't count as company. All the man wanted to do was massage the legs he couldn't feel and force him to take deep breaths.

There were a few regular nurses besides Donovan. They adjusted his position every two hours but made it clear they weren't in his room to talk or swap stories. They also apparently believed they could only do their best work after they'd awakened him from a deep sleep.

He nicknamed the surliest nurse Atilla. He'd seen her interact with the other nurses and doctors, and she seemed pleasant enough with them. But when she talked to him, which wasn't often, she was usually abrupt and unfriendly.

Like Smitty.

Good old Smitty, he snorted. During a bout of desperation, he thought that even a verbal sparring match with him might have helped alleviate the boredom.

He squelched that thought immediately. He didn't want to think about Smitty. Smitty made him think about the ship. The ship made him think about Drew. He did everything he could to not think about Drew.

With an exaggerated sigh, he looked up at the ceiling. He'd already counted the tiles twice today. Once more couldn't hurt. For more of a challenge, he started with the third tile from the left—the one with the crack that looked like an *S*—when Nurse Donovan came in, carrying a tray.

"Hey, Donny," he greeted her, relieved.

"Lunchtime," she announced. "I saw the dietitian in the hallway and told her I'd bring it to you." She laid the tray on the adjustable table and swung it across his chest. Assessing his position in bed, she said, "I think you're high enough. Mind if I join you? I'm on break."

"Glad for the company," he said. "I'm going stir bugs." He lifted the lid off the first plate and curled his lip. "What's that?"

"Canned meat," she apologized.

He scowled. "This is the thanks I get for giving my legs for my country?"

"Now, don't you wish you were back on the ship? You guys got real food. We get rationed spam."

"On *Yorker*, we always made fun of the food."

"Don't you feel guilty?" She lifted the other two lids. "Boiled potatoes. No butter, sorry. Green beans, bread, and chicory. Yum!"

"You know something?" he grinned. "I like you."

"That's because we're a lot alike. It's just that in this job, I have to tamp it down. Believe me, talking to you is a breath of fresh air."

She reached into her uniform pocket and withdrew an envelope. "You got mail today."

Jack nearly choked on the food. "From Loretta?"

"No, but you don't need mail from her. She should be here soon."

Jack whooped.

Atilla poked her head in the doorway. "Keep it down," she snapped. "There are sick people here."

When she left, Jack mimicked her like a six-year-old.

Donovan hid her mouth with her hand. "I wish I could do that."

"Why can't you?"

She dropped her hand. "She's my supervisor."

"Did you say Loretta's coming?"

"Uh-huh. She called this morning and said she'll be here in a few days."

Jack's face fell. "Oh. Not today, though."

"Sorry."

"It's okay. As long as she's coming."

"You did get a letter, though."

She handed him the long envelope.

"Who would write m-" he froze when he saw the name on the envelope.

"Everything okay?" Donovan asked, concerned.

Jack glanced up at her. "Uh, yeah. Sure. Everything's okay." He hesitated. "Letter from a shipmate."

Donovan stood. "Okay, I'll let you read it in private. If you need me, you know where I am."

"Thanks," Jack murmured, without really hearing.

He stared at the envelope for several minutes, unsure whether to open it or just set it aside. The man had saved his life twice. He'd saved Loretta, too.

He slid a finger under the flap and withdrew the single-page handwritten letter.

Hey, meathead, the letter read. *It's your best pal Smitty, ha-ha. I found out what hospital they shipped you to, so I just thought I'd drop a note. They transferred me to the San Diego Naval Base, so now I'm firing off memos instead of guns. Big joke!*

I see your girl's picture in the papers every day. That USO show got everybody's attention Stateside. People in the office keep slapping my back because I got her off the island. One guy even saluted me. Can you believe that?

They said I'm gonna get a medal for that. I already got the Navy Commendation for helping you out when the hellcat hit the deck that day. That and a nickel will get me a cup of coffee.

No fooling, though. If you ask me, it's your pal Brackman who should get the medals and a lot of them. I bet his folks will get one for him soon. There's some talk around here about him getting the Navy Cross, how about that?

It's like I told you on the ship, that Kid had a lot of guts. I've been thinking about what he said about God and the Bible. Peterson told me that Brackman talked to him, too, and he believed everything Brackman told him. One time, I heard Brackman talking to you about that ticket thing when you didn't know I was listening. If Brackman and Peterson believed it, I might have to look into it.

Well, look, I'm going to close here 'cause I have to get back to making paper airplanes. If you ever want to write me, that's fine. If you don't, that's fine, too. Maybe it's best we cut ties and stop remembering the past.

Take care of yourself, buddy. Get back on your feet soon.

Your pal, Smitty.

Chapter Twenty-Four

At night, San Diego glittered like a West Coast version of New Orleans. Brightly lit restaurants and bars situated off busy sidewalks enticed their clientele inside with the sounds of jazz and big band music. Sailors at liberty from the nearby Naval Base and civilians who lived and worked nearby mingled on the sidewalks. They smoked, laughed, and jostled at one another to get into the best places with the best music.

The menus lacked variety, but the drinks were plentiful. With good music, most people didn't mind that braised chicken with root vegetables and chicory was the best meal offered.

Downtown was in stark contrast to the San Diego Bay, only a few miles away. The docks were heavily guarded and dark, with only enough light for laborers and vessels to navigate and work.

One part of the city was half cloaked in war. The other was trying hard to forget it.

Smitty couldn't forget it. On the nights he left the base, he sometimes wandered by the docks, careful not to get too close so that security didn't harass him.

The dim white and yellow bulbs attached to pylons, floating wharves, and wood poles created small circles of light on the rough-hewn boards, but only enough to suggest where someone should walk without tripping.

Navy guards created menacing real-life shadows in the darkness as the hypnotizing sound of the wash slapped and ebbed against pilings.

Smitty always stayed long enough to nourish his depression. Then, when he was sure most people were already in town and the trolley was less crowded, he went into the city for dinner.

Tivoli Bar and Grill on Sixth Avenue was his haunt of choice. The place was old enough to be a favorite of the old-time gunslinger, Wyatt Earp. There was still enough humanity left in Smitty's soul for him to find that amusing.

The bar was rustic, bare bones, furnished with simple wooden tables and chairs, but it had a warm and inviting atmosphere and a history that drew people.

Tonight, though, it was quiet, with only a few there.

Smitty took his usual secluded place at the back. There was a one-page menu on the table, but like all other places, it didn't offer much. It didn't matter. The server knew what he wanted.

Without asking, the waiter brought a mug of cold beer and put it in front of him. Smitty didn't know his name. He didn't want to.

"You want the usual baked fish with vegetables?" the waiter asked.

"That'll do," Smitty said.

The waiter turned to leave, then hesitated and turned back. "You mind if I ask you a question?"

"I mind," Smitty grunted.

The waiter ignored him. "Aren't you the guy that everybody says saved that girl out on the beach not so long ago? Then how come some people say the guy who saved her got killed?"

Smitty stood, reached into his pocket, and threw a bill on the table. "Keep the change. Forget the fish."

He pushed past the startled man as he left.

The sidewalk was still more crowded than he liked, but he could walk it without bumping into anyone. The part of him that still felt alive wished he could enjoy the city more. It was a fun place to be. Part of him wanted to join in, but another part asked why he should bother.

He'd had fun once. Friends and family, too. But the family didn't write much. The magazine they'd sent him on the ship with Loretta's picture on the cover was the first time he'd heard from them in a year. As for friends—

He snorted. His friends somehow all wound up dead. His shipmates on *Valor Bay* were gone. Unger was gone. Peterson was gone. Even little Brackman was gone.

But Jackson was still alive.

The irony that it was Jackson, of all people, that he wanted to talk to now made him laugh out loud. A few passersby eyed him curiously.

He sat on a bench at the curb, braced his elbows on his knees, and laced his fingers under his chin. He watched people laugh, and walk, and talk, and jump on trolley cars. They shook hands, told jokes, and swapped stories. How could they be so casual? Didn't they realize there were kids half a world away giving up their futures so people could go to Tivoli Bar and Grill and lift a mug? Didn't they know that none of it mattered?

He thought again about Brackman. The Kid was no different from any of the rest of them, yet he was. Brackman had thanked him for the shabby trick he'd pulled on him during the wog ceremony, and no matter how hard he'd tried to make the Kid mad by ragging him about his beliefs, Brackman never seemed to mind.

Smitty stood and trudged back towards his trolley stop. He thought about what he'd written to Jackson in the letter. The Kid had something. It wasn't religion. He'd seen enough religious people to know the difference.

Whatever it was, he wanted to know.

The trolley clanged to a stop, and Smitty climbed aboard on his way back to the barracks.

Chapter Twenty-Five

Loretta collapsed into bed immediately after arriving at the hotel in Newark.

Her usual evening routine was to bathe and methodically remove her makeup before spending at least half an hour brushing her teeth, applying skin lotion, brushing her hair, and then gently slipping between the sheets.

This evening, as soon as the hotel room door closed behind her, she unbuttoned her dress and let it fall around her feet in a heap. She slipped out of her heels and kicked the dress away. Clad in her slip and underclothing, she fell into bed.

She was asleep in minutes.

She awakened at noon the next day when the phone on the nightstand beside her bed jangled.

"Mrs. Truett," a female voice on the other end said. "This is room service. We didn't see you at breakfast this morning or receive a call. Would you like us to bring up a breakfast or lunch tray?"

Loretta ran her hand through her hair and let her head fall back against the pillow. "Breakfast would be fine," she sighed. "Can you just leave it in the hallway outside my door? Add a twenty percent tip to my tab."

"Thank you, Ma'am, that's very generous. What would you like us to bring?"

"I'll let you decide," she said. "Nothing too heavy, please." She hesitated. "You don't have coffee, by any chance?"

"We do for you, ma'am."

"Thank you." She hung up the phone and reluctantly climbed out of bed. For a minute, she sat on the edge of the mattress. *I made the right choice to take this day for myself*, she thought. *I can't keep up this pace. How am I going to handle all of this?*

She carted her suitcase into the bathroom and looked in the mirror over the sink. Her haggard face shocked her. "Who are *you*?" she demanded of the reflection. "Who let you into my room?"

She withdrew a jar of Pond's cold cream from her case and removed the previous night's makeup. After splashing water on her face and brushing her teeth, she felt better.

She changed her lingerie, dug a comfortable pair of slacks, flat shoes, and a simple blouse out of the suitcase, and finished up just as a knock sounded on the door.

"Your tray is outside the door, Mrs. Truett," a male voice said on the other side. "I'll just leave it right here."

She didn't answer. A few seconds later, she heard his footfalls recede.

Loretta opened the door when she was sure he was gone. There were two newspapers on the floor. She ignored them. The silver tray beside them held a full pot of coffee and a serving dish covered by a warming top.

"A full pot of coffee," she marveled, bringing the tray in. "Now I know I've made it."

The kitchen had prepared scrambled eggs with toast and jelly, and fried potatoes. It wasn't sumptuous, but lately, nothing was. The government rationed everything. She was just grateful the kitchen had gone above and beyond with the coffee.

She moved the phone from the nightstand to the floor and placed the tray in its place. She then climbed back into bed, on top of the covers, poured a cup of coffee, and moved the plate of eggs onto her lap.

As the meal and especially the coffee revived her, she reflected on her visit to the Studio. After the nightmare of the last several weeks, stepping onto the soundstage had been like being in heaven.

So much fantasy and make-believe, all in one wonderful spot. Colorful costumes, beautiful people, and most wonderful of all, meeting Franklin Meadows.

It was like opening one of the fan magazines from her childhood and stepping into the pages, just like a Disney cartoon. *I'm Snow White, lost in the forest, trying to find my way out*, she thought.

She grimaced, thinking about her task ahead. *Poor, beautiful Jack. So much going for him. Now it's all gone.* The thought of breaking the bad news to him, now only a few hours away, washed away her daydreams like ink in water.

"None of this is fair," she protested aloud. "Why is this happening to me? How am I going to tell him about accepting the movie roles while he's lying there, probably crippled for the rest of his life?"

She remembered Les's assurance from a few days past: *Jack's in the business. He'll understand.*

She poured another cup of coffee.

***

On the evening before Loretta's visit, Jack requested a haircut. His dark hair was trimmed to Navy standards by the on-site barber.

"I need to wear the crackerjack tunic tomorrow," he instructed Atilla as she came in to check his vitals and change his dressings.

The nurse cocked a disdainful eyebrow. "How do you expect me to give you injections or a saline drip through the long sleeves?"

Jack scowled. "How about a white tee, at least? I don't want my girl seeing me in a hospital gown."

"I'll see," Atilla said as she turned to leave.

"Have somebody bring me a razor and a can of Burma Shave in the morning, too," he called after her. "I'll shave myself."

"Too messy," she said. "The barber will do it for you in the morning, as usual." She beat a hasty retreat to deprive him of the last word.

"Too bad she wasn't in the Pacific," he muttered. "The Japanese would have surrendered by now. What's her beef?"

The day dragged by interminably. Even a lunchtime visit by Donovan and the routine of therapy and meals didn't speed up time.

Morphine put him to sleep that night, but his rest was fitful.

Daylight brought breakfast, the barber for a shave, and another therapy session. He endured it all with thinly veiled impatience, but he knew Loretta's visit was close when Donovan brought in the white tee.

She helped him out of the hospital gown and into the shirt. His back injuries made it impossible for him to manage it by himself. She adjusted the sheets around him.

"There." She stepped back. "You look almost human again."

"Almost?"

"Well, compared to what you looked like when you first came in, yeah. And stop worrying. You're as nervous as a kid on a blind date."

"First time we've been together since I've been trussed up like a Thanksgiving turkey."

"Not true. She sat right here beside your bed not so long ago."

"Doesn't count. I didn't know it."

A commotion in the hallway caused them to exchange glances. "It's showtime, Mr. Broadway," Donovan said.

Seconds later, Loretta appeared in the doorway. She wore a smart blue and white suit, her hair pulled back with a clip.

She was the most beautiful sight Jack had ever seen, including the time he'd first met her at the wrap party years earlier.

They stared at one another, neither of them speaking or reacting.

"Um," Donovan prompted. "Do you two need an introduction?"

Loretta swept into the room and stooped beside his bed. Dropping her purse on the floor, she put her white-gloved hands on either side of his face and kissed him.

"I'll just be out in the hallway if anyone needs me," Donovan grinned. As she left, she grabbed the arms of two curious Red Cross volunteers standing at the door and propelled them out.

Jack returned Loretta's kiss with all the longing that had built inside for years. It was the same kiss she remembered that had made her fall in love with him.

She pulled away reluctantly, laughing and crying at the same time. She sat in the chair beside his bed and took his hand. "I can't believe this is happening! Oh, look, my lipstick's all over you!" She took a handkerchief from her purse and wiped red lipstick from his face.

For a moment, he couldn't speak. "Honey," he finally managed. "If this is what it took to get me back to you, it's worth it."

She laughed through fresh tears. "Don't say that."

"I mean it." He squeezed her hand. "Only one rule today—no mention of the USO show, the battle, or any of this." He gestured at his legs. "Just us. Deal?"

"Deal." She brushed a strand of hair from his forehead.

"How's the kid?"

"He misses you like mad. You're all he talks about."

Jack chuckled. "He doesn't even know me. He was a baby when I left."

"He was four years old, and he remembers you very well. He's so proud of you being in the Navy. He's got his whole class convinced you're in charge of the fleet."

He raised his eyebrows. "You mean, I'm not?"

She kissed him again. There was so much to tell him. She didn't know where to start.

She broke the kiss and sat back in the chair.

He searched her face. "You look like the cat who swallowed the canary. What're you thinking?"

She sighed. "It's nothing. It's just that a lot has happened."

She told him about the night she'd left the note, how she'd been diverted to Los Angeles instead of going straight home. "And I've been offered two film roles with Franklin Meadows," she said. "They're just small parts, but they say if I do well, they might offer me a contract."

His face lit. "Franklin Meadows? Honey, that's great! I knew you'd make it big someday."

She wilted with relief. "I'm so glad to hear you say that. I was afraid you'd be upset."

"Why would I be upset?"

"Because it means I'll be in California while you're recovering here."

His smile faded. "I didn't think about that."

"But the studio's arranging flights every month so I can visit," she added. "We'll have a few days together each time."

"A few days." He nodded. "Well, I guess that's something."

"It's not ideal, I know, but—"

He squeezed her hand. "No, it's great news. Really. I want this for you." His expression brightened. "Hey, maybe when I'm back on my feet, we can work together. Ginger and Fred, how about that? I'll have to teach you a few steps, of course."

The words hit her like a blow. Her smile froze.

He sensed her discomfort. "What is it? What's wrong?"

She gave a nervous half-laugh. "Why would you think anything's wrong?"

"Well, either something's wrong, or someone turned a switch off in your brain. You just froze like a rabbit."

She shook her head and stood, snatching her purse from the floor. "No, darling, it's nothing. Don't be concerned. I just—I just need a moment. I have to powder my nose. I'll be right back." She leaned down and kissed his forehead. "*Right* back."

"I'm not going anywhere," he promised.

She hurried from the room.

He stared after her, wondering what had just happened.

Loretta walked towards Leesburg's office as quickly as her spiked heels would allow on the linoleum floor. A few people whispered as they recognized her, but nobody approached.

"Is he in?" Loretta asked Atilla, who was just coming out of a room near Leesburg's office.

Atilla looked toward Jack's room. "Why? Does he need something in there?"

"He's fine," Loretta said. "But I have to talk to Dr. Leesburg right away."

Atilla gave her a quizzical look. She rapped on Leesburg's office door, then opened it without waiting for a response. "Doctor, Mrs. Truett is here. She says she needs to speak with you."

"Send her in," she heard Leesburg say.

Atilla opened the door wider. Loretta pushed past her into the room, her face flushed.

Leesburg nodded at Atilla. "Close the door, please."

The nurse reluctantly complied.

"You haven't told him," Leesburg said. It wasn't a question.

"I can't," she said desperately. "I thought I could, but I can't."

"I see." Leesburg stood. "Stay here, please."

When he left, Loretta sank into the chair in front of his desk and put her head in her hands. She tried to imagine what Jack's reaction might be, but couldn't.

Leesburg returned ten minutes later.

Loretta stood to meet him.

"I informed him," he told her. "He doesn't accept it, but at least he knows."

She twisted her hands. "Is there anything you think I should say to him?"

"That's between the two of you."

Loretta hesitated, thanked him, and left his office, closing the door behind her.

In the hallway, she braced her back against his closed door, oblivious to the curious stares. After a moment, she walked like a condemned woman to Jack's room.

His head was turned, face toward the wall, when she entered.

"Jack," she whispered.

He turned to look at her, his face expressionless.

She didn't move from the doorway. "I'm so sorry, darling. I didn't know how to tell you."

His expression barely shifted. "I wouldn't have known how, either, if I'd been you."

She walked to the chair beside his bed and sat. "What did the doctor say?"

He smirked. "He said I might walk again someday, but they're not sure." His tone was so unemotional that it frightened her.

"Jack—"

"He said they'll be weaning me off the morphine in a while because the fighting men need it, but that I'll get used to the pain." He snorted. "Ironic." His eyebrows rose. "Oh, but here's the good part. He's recommending that the Navy retire me. That's one good thing, at least."

They sat in silence for a minute, then Jack said, "I don't buy any of it."

She took his hand and laced her fingers through his.

They barely spoke the rest of the afternoon.

***

Loretta stayed for the allotted two days, but there wasn't an hour she didn't want to leave. After the doctor's revelation, Jack withdrew. He talked, but without substance, as though he was afraid he'd reveal too much if he opened his mouth.

Whether his refusal to talk was Navy bravado, fear, or pride, Loretta wasn't sure, but it was as if their joyous reunion had never happened.

"I'm sorry," he apologized as she kissed him goodbye on the last day. "This isn't the way I wanted our first meeting to go after all these years."

"You have nothing to apologize for," she assured him. "It's a shock. I love you. Next time I come, there'll be no new surprises. We'll start all over again." She ruffled his thick hair. "I'm afraid you're stuck with me for the rest of your life, my dear."

He snorted softly. "I think that's my line."

Chapter Twenty-Six

Kenny Bachmann, the director of *The Burden of the Day*, hated working with Franklin Meadows.

Despite recent slides at the box office, the veteran actor was respected. He'd been the Studio's bread and butter for years.

In the 1930s, he'd almost always played a swashbuckler. As the decade passed, he took on more serious roles, effortlessly manipulating the nuances of each role with the deftness of a skilled artist.

He also never accepted direction. Worse, he tended to direct other actors who appeared in his scenes, making Bachmann and any other director who worked with him feel irrelevant.

The Studio turned a deaf ear to the directors' complaints. They were still willing to make concessions for him. At least for the time being.

Bachmann watched from across the soundstage as Loretta entered, looking slightly bewildered. For her role as Meadows's secretary, she wore an ordinary tweed business suit with brown wedge heels. Her hair was pulled back in a partial bun with the sides fastened by barrettes at her temples.

She even makes that get-up look good, Bachmann thought, impressed. *At least they didn't get too corny and give her glasses. If Meadows is wrapped up with her, I might actually get a chance to direct my own movie for a change.*

He feigned a wide, amiable grin as she approached. "Nice to meet you, Mrs. Truett." He extended a hand. "I'm Kenny Bachmann, the director of the film."

Loretta smiled and shook his hand. "Very glad to meet you." She glanced nervously around the busy set, accidentally catching the eye of Meadows's leading lady, Marinell Tyler.

The actress was ten years older than Loretta, but beautiful. Her famously sculpted high cheekbones, aristocratic long nose, and elaborate false eyelashes gave her the look of an animated Egyptian goddess. She wore silk lounging pajamas and a matching robe for her part. It was the type of outfit Loretta would have worn better in a fashion shoot.

Loretta smiled at her and waved.

Marinell rolled her eyes and walked in the opposite direction.

Well, you're off to a great start, girl, Loretta thought. *I've always liked her so much in the movies. I hope she'll warm up to me as we get to know one another.*

She looked at Bachmann. "I thought there might be a reading or run-through before we actually start shooting."

"We've already done that." Bachmann put a hand on her upper back, steering her across the stage. "Your role is minor. We didn't think you needed to be in on those." He led her around the cables and similar perils of shooting that were scattered like snakes across the floor.

"You've already met our star, I think," Bachmann said as he motioned to Meadows, who was talking to a technician a few feet away.

Meadows's eyes lit as he saw her. "Loretta, my little love!" He came toward her with a toothy grin. "I've been waiting for you to arrive!" He embraced her, then pulled back and held her at arm's length. "If this is what secretaries look like in the business world today, I've been in the wrong profession! You look lovely."

"Thank you, Frank. I'm a little nervous."

"You won't be once we get started." He looked at Bachmann. "Isn't that right, Kenny?"

"If you say so," Bachmann said. "You always know best, Frank. Why don't you find a quiet place somewhere for a few minutes and go over Loretta's lines with her?"

"I'd love to," Meadows said. He hooked his arm through Loretta's and led her toward the far end of the sound stage. "Let's find a spot and do a little rehearsing, why don't we?"

"I'd appreciate it," she said.

"So would I," Bachmann muttered as he watched them go.

Marinell approached him. "So, that's her, huh?" She watched Loretta and Meadows sit in a private alcove on an empty set. "Little Miss War Hero."

"Yeah," Bachmann said. He picked up a script from a sawhorse and flipped through a few pages. "Shame what happened to her."

"Yeah," Marinell snorted. "She looks all torn up."

Bachmann didn't look up from his script. "She's handling it better than I probably would."

Marinell squinted, scrutinizing the model across the room. "She's not all that pretty close up, is she?"

Bachmann gave her an incredulous look. "You're joking, right?"

***

After work that night, Meadows drove Loretta home to the temporary house the studio had provided—a charming four-bedroom mock Tudor cottage, tucked behind an impenetrable security fence.

The man in the guard's booth recognized them as Meadows drove up. He hurried from his cage to open the gates.

"How did you get us here without being followed?" Loretta asked Meadows. "Lately, I can't go anywhere without a pack of people screaming questions at me and taking pictures."

"I simply won't put up with their nonsense," he explained as he drove through the security gate. "I've been around so long, they all know it's best not to harass me. I'm respected in this industry, and for good reason. I've been the Studio's number one draw for many years."

He navigated the roundabout to the front steps of the house and left the motor running.

"Would you like to come in for a few minutes?" she asked. "My son Russell is probably still awake. It's so hard to get him into bed on time. We've seen your movies together. I'm sure he'd love to meet you."

He frowned. "I forgot you have a child. I remember reading the newspaper articles when you married Moe Truett." He gave her a mildly incredulous look. "Whatever made you walk away from a man that powerful? He's got all of Broadway in the palm of his hand."

She bristled. "I didn't walk away. He divorced me when he found out I was expecting. He's never even seen Russell, although the child support and alimony keep coming."

"Well, at least he's decent enough to provide for you."

"Oh, please. He knows I'll sue him into oblivion if those checks don't come every month." She laughed self-consciously. "I'm sorry. Sour grapes. Don't get me going. Would you like to come in?"

"Thank you," he said.

When they entered the foyer, Russell, dressed in white sailor suit pajamas, burst from a back room with his studio-hired nanny not far behind. "Mommy!" he flew into her arms, throwing his arms around her neck.

"Hello, Admiral!" she said, pulling back to peck his cheek with a kiss.

"Did you bring me something?"

"Well, let me see." She put him down, reached into her purse, and withdrew a pack of chewing gum. "How about this?"

"Oh, boy!" he snatched it from her and plopped down at her feet to rip open the package.

"Will you need me any longer this evening, Mrs. Truett?" the nanny asked.

"No, thank you so much," Loretta said. "Was he good for you?"

"He's a handful," the nanny grinned, "But a fun handful. Goodnight, Miss. I'll be back at six o'clock tomorrow morning."

"Thanks, Anna."

When the door closed behind her, Loretta stooped to address Russell. "Stand up, sweetheart, and be polite. I want you to meet my friend, Mr. Meadows."

Russell stuffed a stick of gum in his mouth and peered up at Meadows. "Are you in the Navy?"

Meadows was taken aback. He laughed. "Well, not directly. I played the captain of a pirate ship, once. Does that count?"

Russell jumped to his feet, excited. "You're the captain of a pirate ship?"

"Mr. Meadows is an actor, honey," Loretta explained. "You and I went to the movies and saw him in the pirate movie, remember?"

Russell didn't make the connection. "My Uncle Jack is in the Navy," he said.

"So, I've heard," Meadows said.

"Yep! He's the boss of the whole Navy. He's got his own ship, too."

"Is that right?"

"Yep, and he's got lots of medals, and he's going to give me one." He thought a moment. "He's in the hospital right now, so he can't come home. He's got a broken arm. But pretty soon, he'll come home, and then he won't be my uncle anymore. He'll be my daddy!" He jumped up and down. "Yea! Yea!"

"All right, calm down," Loretta said. "You're all dressed for bed, so scoot on in there."

"I want to stay and talk to the pirate."

"The pirate will talk to you another time when it's not almost two hours past your bedtime."

She led her protesting son down the hallway into his room.

Meadows sighed and shook his head. He'd been married twice but had no children. The very thought was exhausting.

He glanced around the room. Though Loretta had occupied the cottage for only a few days, she'd already added personal touches.

He walked to the window ledge where framed photos perched. There were a few of Russell at various ages. Most were of Loretta and the man whose identity he didn't have to guess at.

"That's Jack," Loretta said behind him.

He turned, slightly startled. "So sorry! I didn't hear you!"

She handed him a goblet of wine. "Why don't we sit down?"

"Thank you." He looked back at the photographs again before joining her on the sofa. "You said he was an entertainer before the war?"

She nodded.

"He looks it."

"He'd just finished a successful show on Broadway when the war started. It took him a lot of hard work to reach that goal, but he finally got there."

"And now, there's no chance?" he asked.

She shook her head. "I just returned from visiting him in the hospital. His doctor gave him the news while I was there."

"How did he take it?"

She laughed shortly. "I wish I knew. He stopped talking. I guess that's how he took it."

"What are your plans now?"

"I can't think that far ahead. He's got months of surgeries and rehabilitation. After that—" she shrugged fatalistically. "I guess we'll see." She raised her glass. "In the meantime, I make movies with tiny little roles and try not to think about it."

He swished the liquid in the goblet, then clinked his glass against hers. "You were very good today. Your roles won't be small for long. The Studio may be capitalizing on your USO mishap and magazine covers right now, but they didn't hire you to be in films with a name like me because they're shortsighted."

He chuckled. "Marinell's face was so red, even through all that makeup, I thought she'd have a stroke!" He raised his eyebrows. "That's a good sign. She knows you're going places. So do I."

He laid his glass aside. "Loretta, I know what you're up against, but if today was any indication, and I believe it was, you have a future in this godforsaken business. Don't let it get away from you."

"Jack should come first," she said. She laid her glass aside and stood. "Frank, I hope you won't think me rude, but would you mind if we called it a night? Tomorrow comes very early."

He blinked, startled. He couldn't remember ever being asked to leave an attractive woman's home. "Of course," he said when he recovered. He stood. “Would you like me to pick you up in the morning?”

She looked at him uncertainly. “Well, I—"

“I know how to avoid the press.”

“Then yes!” she exclaimed with a short laugh. “By all means.”

He grinned and leaned forward to brush her cheek with a kiss. “I’ll see you at six o’clock in the morning. I’ll just show myself out.”

When he had gone and she heard the engine of his car start in the driveway, she sat on the sofa, confused. Was he being nice, or was he flirting like a good movie star was expected to?

“Don’t be ridiculous," she tsked. "He’s old enough to be your father.” Moe Truett had been, too. She wouldn't make that mistake again.

Besides, she was engaged to Jack.

Chapter Twenty-Seven

For a week after Loretta left for Los Angeles, Jack couldn't stop replaying his mistakes. Those years at sea, enduring the stress of battle and the sweatbox the Navy called a ship, had been fueled by one thought—being with her. That dream had kept him sane, kept him from jumping overboard. He'd ruined it in minutes.

Congratulations, Pal, he berated himself. *You turned yourself into a bigger jerk than Smitty.*

First, she'd had the joy of seeing him strung up like a hooked tuna, then she got the great news that she had an invalid on her hands for the rest of her life. And best of all? He'd acted like it was her fault by refusing to talk to her about it.

Donovan interrupted his self-pity by poking her head into his room. "You up to a visitor?"

He raised his brows. "Who?"

"A girl who says you have a mutual friend. We thought she might be another reporter trying to get through, but she doesn't look the type. Does the name Drew ring any bells?"

Jack opened his mouth, then clamped it shut again. His pulse quickened. "Yeah, I knew a guy by the name of Drew. Did she tell you her name?"

Donovan thought. "Um, "Lori, Corrie—"

"Dorrie?"

She snapped her fingers. "That's it. Shall I send her up?"

"Yeah," he said. His voice sounded unnatural to his ears. "Send her up."

He stared at the door with dread and disbelief. The shocks never seemed to end. What was she doing here? Did she have a bone to pick? Did she blame Loretta for Drew's death? Was she mad at him for not keeping the Kid safe?

When Dorrie peeked into the room with a shy smile, his concerns evaporated.

She was more attractive in person than in the picture Drew had shown him. She had dark blonde hair and large blue eyes. She dressed like a teen, though she was too old for the style. She held a simple cloth purse and wore a cotton print dress, bobby socks, and black and white oxfords.

There was still enough pain in her eyes to tell him she wasn't reconciled to Drew's death. He wondered if seeing him was the reason that look was there.

"Hello," she said. "Ya look just like your picture that Loretta showed me at her house that time. I hope I'm not botherin' ya." She took a step into the room. "Is it okay if I come in for a minute?"

Loretta was right. Her accent sounded Brooklyn, but not quite.

He hesitated. He wasn't sure he wanted this kind of reminder so soon. But he didn't want to be rude to Drew's girl, either. "Sure," he said. He indicated the chair beside his bed. "Come in and sit down."

As she sat, she pointed at the pulleys and weights of the traction. "Ya don't look real comfortable."

"I'm getting used to it," he said, trying to lighten the awkward mood. "It's like lounging in a hammock on the beach."

She snorted, smiled a little, and said, "I betcha not." She hesitated, casting for her next words. "I guess ya haven't been outside for a while. It's really hot for this time of year. Unseasonable, the man on the radio said."

He wondered how much small talk she was going to make before she told him why she'd come. "No, I haven't been outside."

"Yeah." She cleared her throat. "Well, listen. I'm really sorry ya got hurt so bad. I felt terrible when I found out. I mean, between you and Drew, one of ya shoulda made it out safe, y'know?"

She looked down at her hands, folded in her lap. "I, um, I'm not gonna stay long. I came by to give ya somethin', 'cause I thought ya might like it, then I'll leave."

She reached into her purse and withdrew something wrapped in fake velvet. "I guess ya know Drew was gonna be a minister after the war."

Jack nodded.

She unwrapped the cloth, her fingers lingering on its edges before she pulled the covering back to reveal a large black book. "Drew wrote to us about ya. We know you two were good friends. His family and I wanted to give ya somethin' that was special to Drew, but we couldn't decide what. We talked about it for days, and this is what we came up with."

She held the book out to him. "This is the Bible that Drew got when he was baptized. It's a little beat up 'cause he used it a lot, but it was the one he used most when he was home. His dad, who died, gave it to him, so he loved it.

"He left it with his mother when he joined the Navy. He said he didn't want anything to happen to it. Now, we want you to have it." She held the book out. "Here."

Jack hesitated, almost afraid to touch it. "You can't give this to me. This is too important to give away."

"Drew would want ya to have it." She held it out again. "It's yours."

He had no choice but to take it.

She leaned forward to kiss his cheek. "That's for bein' Drew's good friend."

Jack had always prided himself on his emotional fortitude, but he was close to losing it now. He hesitated, then beckoned her closer. He returned the kiss to her cheek. "That's from me," he said, then he gave her a light kiss on the lips. "And that's from Drew."

Her eyes flooded. "Oh, thanks," she said, sniffling. The tears escaped and slid down her cheeks. "I guess I'd better go, or I'll be makin' a fool outta myself. I'm sorry I can't stay and talk, 'cause I'd like to." She hesitated. "But I could come again sometime if I'm not intrudin' too much and ya wouldn't mind."

"Do you think it's a good idea?" he asked. "Maybe it's too much remembering for both of us."

She nodded. "Okay. If ya don't want me to, I won't. I hope ya feel better soon, Jack. Our whole church is prayin' for ya."

She was almost out the door when he called her back. "Dorrie."

She peeked back in.

"Listen," he said. "If you want to come sometime, it's okay."

She nodded, smiled, and waved goodbye.

Jack lay his head against the pillow. "What did I just do?" He looked down at the Bible in his hands. "What did you just do, you idiot?"

***

Jack laid the book beside him on the bed. He didn't open it. He'd never touched a Bible in his life. Until he'd met Drew, he'd always thought about religion as superstitious nonsense. Most of the so-called Christians he'd ever met looked down on his profession and his lifestyle. They scowled as often as they breathed, yet were always the first to tell him how happy they were and how much he was missing.

Drew had blown his conceptions. There'd been nothing irrational or judgmental about him. He'd had more character than men twice his age. He handled a deck gun like he'd been born with it in his hands.

Jack remembered the time he'd ragged Drew as a hypocrite for being a gunner. Where did his so-called Christianity go while he was pulling the trigger?

"If somebody broke into my house and tried to kill my family," Drew answered. "I wouldn't stand aside and smile while they did it. That would make me just as much of a killer as they are. That's what it's like out here. I'm not asking the other side to attack us or try to tear down my country. But if being a gunner means protecting Yonkers and taking care of the guys around me, I'll do it."

A startling idea occurred to him. He'd always thought the reason he'd hung out with the kid was to protect him. Here, all along, it might've been the other way around.

He eyed the book warily, hesitant, but couldn't ignore it. What was he afraid of? That it would catch fire in his hands?

With a huff, he snatched it up. Some of the pages were more frayed than others. Those must have been the spots Drew read most. He opened to one of the more ragged pages in the middle.

It looked like a poem. He read the lines that Drew had underlined:

The Lord is my shepherd; I shall not want. He maketh me to lie down in green pastures. He leadeth me beside the still waters. He restoreth my soul. He leadeth me in the paths of righteousness for his name's sake. Yea, though I walk through the valley of the shadow of death, I will fear no evil, for thou art with me. Thy rod and thy staff, they comfort me. Thou preparest a table before me in the presence of mine enemies. Thou anointest my head with oil. My cup runneth over. Surely goodness and mercy shall follow me all the days of my life, and I will dwell in the house of the Lord forever.

It was a poem a fighting man could identify with. It reminded him of the lyrics to the Navy hymn.

Eternal Father, strong to save, whose arm hath bound the restless wave. Who bidd'st the mighty ocean deep, its own appointed limits keep. Oh, hear us when we cry to Thee, for those in peril on the sea! Amen.

He read the next poem in the book and the one that followed. He didn't understand all of the old words or much of the meaning, but there was something gentle about them that quietened him, a feeling he'd not had for a long time.

He turned towards the end of the book to see what else Drew had underlined.

Come unto me, all ye that labour and are heavy laden, and I will give you rest. Take my yoke upon you and learn of me; for I am meek and lowly in heart and ye shall find rest unto your souls. For my yoke is easy, and my burden is light.

He wondered who the words were talking about. He remembered Drew had quoted those lines to him once. He'd scoffed and said if he ever met a guy who claimed to be meek and lowly, he'd tell him to toughen up.

But Drew had been gentle and quiet. He'd also been strong and courageous. Maybe that's what meek and lowly meant. Smitty said Drew had guts, but he wasn't loud and noisy about it.

Jack returned to the poetry book in the middle. Starting at the first poem, he read until it became dark outside, and Atilla came in to check his vitals and change his bandages.

She raised an eyebrow when she saw what he was reading.

"What?" he protested. "A guy can't read the Bible if he wants to?"

"Sure," she said. "I just never thought I'd see you doing it."

He was tempted to ask her if she knew anything about the Bible, and if she knew where the part about the ticket was. But she seemed to be in a particularly prickly mood tonight, which was saying a lot for Atilla. He let it go.

Dorrie was sure to know. He'd ask her next time she came to visit.

Chapter Twenty-Eight

Loretta was no stranger to show business parties. Her marriage to Moe Truett had given her access to the most lavish social bashes on Broadway. She'd hobnobbed with prominent actors, producers, and writers on The Great White Way, all of them decked out in elegant tuxedos and glittering gowns.

When Jack made his prodigious splash on stage, the whirlwind began all over again. She'd been the most beautiful girlfriend on the arm of the most handsome up-and-coming young man in theater.

But nothing could have prepared her for the late Renaissance-themed extravagance of a Samuels Brothers dinner party at Ciro's nightclub.

The gleaming black limousine with privacy shades she shared with Meadows pulled up to the entrance of the famous club. The car was immediately attended to by a white-gloved attendant wearing a red uniform with gold braid at the shoulder. He opened the door of the back seat to allow the couple to emerge.

Franklin Meadows looked dashing and cultured in his white-pleated dress shirt, carnation boutonniere, and black tuxedo with satin lapels.

But it was Loretta who turned heads. Her auburn hair complemented her emerald green gown with spaghetti straps and sequins. Silver spiked heels defined her shapely legs.

As she entered the room on Meadows's arm, even those most accustomed to being fawned over appreciated the new goddess in their midst.

"You're making them look," Meadows whispered as attendants ushered them into Ciro's opulence.

She gave him a *don't be silly* glance, but knew he was right.

"Do you think Moe Truett will be jealous when he sees pictures of you on my arm in tomorrow's trade papers?" he asked.

"Oh," she exclaimed. "I do hope so!"

Ornate carved facades and dramatic woodwork decorated the baroque-themed room. Silk curtains spilled like waterfalls over two raised platforms that would stage big bands later in the evening. Small round tables dressed with white linen tablecloths, napkins, and overturned wine glasses lined the dance area on both sides.

Film stars that Loretta recognized from the movies, and from her short time on the studio lot, occupied the tables. Men and women accustomed to being the center of attention stared as she and Meadows were led toward their table near the dance floor.

Marinell grabbed his arm as they walked past. "Not even going to say hello?"

Frank looked at Loretta. "Go on, darling. You'll find our place by the placards on the table. I'll be right with you."

When she was out of earshot, he turned to Marinell. "Are you having a good time?"

"Not as much as you," she said. "Robbing the cradle again, Frank? Or just hitching your star to someone who's going up instead of down?"

He raised his eyebrows. "Do you know how dreadful you look when you're jealous, dear?"

She smiled. "Maybe, but I console myself with the fact that my box office isn't diving, like someone else I know and love."

He bent down to kiss her cheek. "You're always such a delight."

He was surprised to find Morris Samuels and his wife, Sophia, at their table, flanking Loretta on either side.

"Why, Morris, hello! I didn't know you were joining us tonight." He took his place at the table across from Loretta and extended a hand to Sophia, an attractive, white-coiffed woman of about sixty. "Always a pleasure, Sophie, dear."

She smiled. "Always nice to see you, too, Frank."

"Are we the only four at this table?" Loretta asked. "There are two other empty places."

"It's just the four of us this evening," Samuels said.

The server came by and took their drink orders. When he was gone, Sophia said, "I've been reading about you in the newspapers, Loretta."

Loretta groaned. "Oh, I know. I thought the press would be tired of me by now."

"Not with a story like yours. It almost sounds like a movie script."

Intrigued by the possibility, Samuels raised an eyebrow.

"To think she was just a cover girl not long ago," Meadows said.

"Oh, not just a cover girl," Sophia said. She laid a gloved hand on Loretta's arm. "This girl's got *it*!"

Loretta blushed, uncomfortable with the excessive attention in the room and at the table. It had been fun when the *Marquee Quarterly* cover had come out, but now the more people gushed, the more embarrassed she became.

"How do you like making your first movie?" Samuels asked.

"Very much," she said. "It's helped distract me from less pleasant things. I'm very grateful for the opportunity."

Samuels looked at his wife. "Loretta's fiancé had a promising future on Broadway before the war."

"Yes," Sophia said. "I've seen his picture in the papers. He was quite the talk of the town. And very young, wasn't he?"

"Jack was twenty-one or so at the time," Loretta said, "but he grew up in theater, so he was ready for it."

Sophia's eyebrows ascended. "Indeed? Would I recognize any of his earlier work?"

"No, dear," Samuels said. "He performed an elaborate form of dance and acrobatics with his parents when he was a child on the Lowe's Vaudeville Circuit."

Why am I surprised he knows that? Loretta thought.

"Oh, how wonderful!" Sophia laughed. "I used to love the vaudeville shows." She glanced at her husband. "Do you remember how much fun they were?" She grinned at Loretta. "We used to sneak away from parties so that we could see the acts. I wonder if we ever saw Jack."

Samuels took a sip from his wineglass. "It's possible. The Jackson Family Dancers toured the country, but I don't believe we ever caught that act. Loretta was a vaudeville performer as a child, too."

Meadows shot Loretta a startled look.

Loretta laughed, bothered, but amazed. "Mr. Samuels, you know all the secrets!"

"I have a large portfolio," he smiled. "It's my business to know about the people who work for me. And Sophia's right. Vaudeville was fun. I miss it. It's too bad about Jack."

Meadows tsked. "Yes, such a shame, isn't it? But life moves on, doesn't it?"

Samuels gave him a curious look.

The waiter took their entrée orders, and the talk around the table turned to more pleasantly frivolous matters.

Loretta's wariness of Morris Samuels waned as the evening progressed. After what she considered had been his ambush of her during their initial meeting in his office, she'd felt certain he held her in low esteem. But as the evening passed, he seemed more like the good-natured grandfather of her first impression.

After the entrée, the waiter brought Baked Alaska to their table and flambéed it there.

"This is delightful!" Loretta exclaimed. "I had friends who provided me with baking ingredients from time to time, but this goes far beyond anything I could have made."

The three veteran show people at the table chuckled. Sophia laid a hand on her arm. "You're going to like Wonderland, Alice."

As the band prepared to mount the stage for the after-dinner performance, Samuels turned to Meadows and said, "Will you excuse Loretta and me for a few minutes, Frank?"

"Well, I—" Meadows said, surprised. "Well, yes, of course."

Sophia stood. "I think I'll excuse myself, too, for just a few minutes." She touched the tip of her nose. "My powder needs refreshing."

When they were alone, Samuels said. "I'm going to make this fast because the band will make hearing anything at all impossible in just a moment." He laid a hand on her arm. "I'm impressed with you. The publicity mills are impressed with you. I'm told you're turning that minor role as Frank's secretary into a standout performance by just—well, by just standing there."

"Thank you, sir," Loretta said.

The band tuned up.

"Come by my office tomorrow morning. I'm having the writers enlarge your part in this film. I'm not offering you the moon yet, but I'm ready to sign you for two years. That will give us enough time to tell if all of this is just a flash in the pan or if you really have staying power."

Loretta's hand flew to her mouth.

"The next film you star in after *The Burden of the Day* will be opposite Meadows in a romantic comedy called *Art Deco*. It starts as soon as *Burden* is complete."

The horn intro to "Chattanooga Choo-Choo" sounded.

Samuels tapped her hand. "Tomorrow. We'll discuss more fully."

Chapter Twenty-Nine

A deep, throbbing pain in Jack's lower back awakened him from sleep. Seconds later, he was aware of a burning and tingling sensation radiating through his nerve-damaged legs.

"Donovan!" he yelled.

Atilla entered his room at the sound of his shout, pushing a cart laden with bottles and dressings. Her expression remained clinically neutral as she checked his vitals. With that task completed, she picked up antiseptics and new dressings from the cart.

"Brace yourself, this is going to hurt." She unwrapped the previous night's dressing from his legs.

He swore through clenched teeth when she touched him. With each unwrapped bandage, it felt like she was ripping the skin from his bones.

He clamped down, refusing to surrender to pain. It was the first real discomfort he'd felt since the accident.

When she finished, Atilla reached for a bottle on the tray and tipped two pills into a cup. She put her hand behind his head and dropped the capsules on his tongue.

"What's happening?" he demanded.

"You're being weaned off the morphine in between surgeries," she said. "A little at a time until you adapt. They'll put you back on when you need it after an operation. I just gave you codeine. It's not as strong as morphine, but it'll help."

"How long does this stuff take to work?"

She looked at her watch. "About thirty minutes. I'll be back to check."

At the door, she glanced back, her expression determined and resentful. "I want you to know you're lucky to have a room to yourself. You can thank your girlfriend for that. There are two wards full of men, most in worse shape than you. You're not the only one. None of them has their own room."

He glared. "What are you talking about?"

"You heard me," she said as she left.

God, he prayed inwardly. It was the only prayer he'd ever made. He wasn't sure what to say next.

Thirty minutes passed, and the pain ebbed. Atilla was right. It wasn't the kind of relief he got from morphine, but it was better than unremitting misery.

Exhausted, he let his head fall deeper into the pillow, afraid to fall asleep in case he woke up to the same experience. He closed his eyes and tried to relax while the codeine worked.

A few minutes later, he heard footsteps enter his room. He opened his eyes and mouth at the same time, ready to blister Atilla with what he thought of her. But it was Donovan.

"Why didn't someone warn me?" he demanded.

"We tried, but you weren't listening."

"Don't give me that bull," he snapped. "I'd have remembered something like that."

"Okay," she said. "This isn't the best time for a conversation, I see. I just want you to know that Doctor Leesburg was passing in the hall outside your room when he heard what the nurse said to you. She got a good dressing down, and I thought you might like to know."

"What did she mean that I have a private room because of Loretta? Why should I get special treatment?"

She gestured at the chair. "Mind if I sit?"

He didn't answer.

She sat. "When you first got here, this room was like Grand Central Station. You needed almost round-the-clock care. You were in pretty serious trouble."

"And now I'm not?"

"You're improving. You're beating up on the wrong person here, you know."

He wasn't mollified. "Why do I still have a private room if I'm getting better?"

"That's a little hard to explain."

"Let's start with Loretta getting me special privileges."

"It's not her fault."

"Cut through the baloney, Donovan."

"Okay, Jack, no baloney. After what happened at the USO show, people can't get enough of your young lady."

"There were plenty of other people out there with that show."

"Maybe so, but she was the only civilian caught in the middle of it all. Not only that, she's making a movie. People are interested.

"Right now, all the attention she's getting means we can't put you in with the general population because those wards are on the bottom floors. The press has breached the lobbies more than once, trying to find you. We've had to hire additional security guards. Your room is on the third floor. It's easier to protect."

"That's nuts."

"Well, that's all I can tell you." She stood. "You're good for six hours, my friend. We'll give you another dose before that one wears off. Tonight, we'll give you a nerve block." Her expression softened. "I'm sorry you didn't understand what was coming."

***

Dear Jack, Loretta's letter read. *I was prepared to visit you this week, but I just got a call from the front office. They want me to stay longer because they're expanding my part. They're very happy with my work. They're even giving me a bigger role in this picture! In fact, the second movie I was originally offered was given to someone else. Hold onto your hat, you won't believe this!*

The Studio is signing me! In fact, in a few weeks, they're starring Frank and me together in my first full film. You're not going to believe this, but it's called Art Deco! Yea! My favorite thing. Ugh! I wonder if that's an omen?

I know that none of this would have happened without Frank. He's been a good friend. I can't wait to introduce him to you. I think the two of you will really hit it off. Never in my wildest dreams would I have believed this could happen.

Do you know what this contract with the Studio means? When we're finally married, we'll be living in sunny California. No unnecessary aches and pains as you recover because of cold weather.

Sadly, I had to let my long-time manager, Les Holt, go. The Studio says he's no longer necessary. Les was terribly disappointed, and I hated to hurt him. He's a dear soul. But sometimes it's necessary to make hard decisions.

Don't bother writing back, Dear. I will probably be in the air on my way to you, just as your letter reaches my house next week.

Russell wants to know where the medals are!

Love, Loretta.

Chapter Thirty

Dorrie stood in the doorway to Jack's room. She wore a pink waitress uniform and held a small paisley cloth satchel.

"I know it's only been a few weeks since the last time I came," she said. "But I brought somethin' I thought ya'd like to see. Is it okay if I come in?"

Jack was glad to see her. "Sure, it is." He motioned her inside the room. "Make yourself at home."

She crossed the floor and sat in the wooden folding chair beside his bed. She put the satchel on the floor, indicating the traction unit with a tilt of her head. "How long 'til you're outta that contraption?"

"Not sure," Jack said. "The bones are setting. A few other things are going on in there, too."

"Like what?"

"Crushed muscles and nerves."

She winced. "Just one-a those woulda been enough, dontcha think?"

He snorted. "No kidding. What's in the bag? Another present?"

"Why, I bet ya haven't even finished the last present I brought."

"Give me a break. It's a big book."

She nodded. "I'll say. Drew and me—excuse me, Drew and *I*—read it straight through before he joined the Navy."

"The whole thing? From the top, you mean?"

"Uh-huh."

"That thing's almost as big as the phone book."

"It took us a year, but we did it. We were so proud, we went to MacGiver's drugstore and got banana splits with nuts."

"And whipped cream?"

"What else? And before ya ask—cherry on top."

Jack chuckled.

She reached down and fingered the strings of the satchel.

He thought she was about to divulge its secrets, but she still wasn't ready.

"What comes next?" she asked, straightening. "For you, I mean?"

"Back surgery. Not sure when. They're waiting on other things to patch up first."

"I'm sorry," she said. "When ya get hurt, ya don't do it halfway. I bet Loretta bein' here helps a lot."

He snorted. "If I'm lucky, I might find out someday."

She missed the nuance. "She's gettin' so famous, it's crazy! She came by the counter before she went to the USO show. Now everybody thinks I'm her best pal."

"You mean she hasn't contacted you?"

She looked baffled. "No, why should she?" She realized what he meant in the next second. Her eyes widened, and her mouth formed an understanding oval.

"You mean because of what Drew did?" She shook her head. "No, I haven't heard from her, but I understand. She probably doesn't know what to say." She hesitated. "Loretta sent back the envelope I gave her for Drew, though."

"What envelope?"

"I gave her an envelope full of letters from me and his folks to give him at the show. She sent a note with it that said they were on the way back to the boat to get it when—" She hesitated. "We're gettin' into places I don't want to go right now, okay?"

"Okay," he quickly agreed.

"Anyway," she continued, "now people at work think I have the inside scoop on Hollywood. The only scoop I know is putting vanilla ice cream in cones."

He laughed. "All right, but enough procrastinating. What's in the bag? You said you had something to show me."

She picked up the tote at her feet. "I had to promise Drew's mother on a stack of Bibles that I'd take good care of this and bring it home safe and sound." She opened the satchel and withdrew a rectangular black box with a gold-embossed Navy seal on top.

Jack recognized it immediately. He'd received two similar boxes just days earlier. "Is that Drew's?"

"Uh-huh." She opened the box, revealing a bronze cross with rounded edges, four laurel leaves with berries, and an ancient sailing ship cresting the waves at the center. "Here." She gently lifted the precious medal from the case by its blue and white ribbon. She held it out to him. "Look on the back."

Respectfully, Jack took Drew's Navy Cross. "It's great," he murmured. "Nobody deserves it more."

"Turn it over," she suggested again. "It's pretty on that side, too."

He carefully turned the medal on his palm. Crossed anchors with cables were etched on the back in relief, with the letters USN in the center.

For a minute, he gazed at it, recalling a wog roast and shared battles, talks about God, and a few heated arguments.

She didn't interrupt his reverie.

After a few minutes, he passed it back to her. "Thank Drew's mom for letting you bring it. Thank yourself, too."

"He got the Purple Heart, too," she said.

She put the medal back in the box, closed the top, and kissed it before returning it to the bag. "I don't know if I did either one of us any good by doin' that." She retrieved a hanky from the pocket of her uniform and swiped her eyes. "But I thought Drew would like ya to know he got it, seein' how you two were good friends."

"Thanks, honey," Jack said.

She took a deep breath, waited a few seconds to compose herself, then said. "How about we change the subject?"

"How about we do that?" He hesitated, wanting to ask questions about Drew's Bible, but afraid of being lectured. He decided to jump overboard. "Listen, about the gift you brought last time. Just how much do you know about the Bible, anyway?"

"I was gonna be a minister's wife. I'd say I know more than most."

"Mind if I ask a few questions?"

"Shoot."

"I've been flipping through Drew's Bible looking for where it talks about the ticket, but I can't find it. Where is that?"

Her face blanked. "The what?"

"The ticket. Drew talked about a ticket that gets you into heaven. Like, you can't get into a show without giving the ticket to the usher."

She stared at him, mystified, then her face lit with abrupt understanding. "Oh, *that* ticket!"

"Yeah. The way you hesitated, I thought Drew might've made it up."

She laughed. "No, he didn't make it up. That sounds like a story he'd tell to make it easier for people to understand. Oh, yeah, the ticket's all over the place, but especially in John 3:16."

He picked the heavy book up from the table and handed it to her. "Show me."

She took the Bible from his hands and immediately turned to the passage.

"You knew right where to turn," Jack said, impressed.

"Don't give me too much credit," she scoffed. "Everybody knows where to find John 3:16."

He decided not to challenge that.

"Here," she said, holding the book out to him. "Do you wanna read it?"

"You go 'head."

"Okay."

She read:

"For God so loved the world, that he gave his only begotten Son, that whosoever believeth in him, should not perish, but have everlasting life. For God sent not his Son into the world to condemn the world, but that the world through Him might be saved."

She looked up. "So, there you go. There's the ticket."

"I've never believed," he said. "Especially after the last few years, seeing some of the stuff I have. I'm not sure I ever could. But if anyone could make me think about it, it's Drew." He hesitated. "And you."

Her face reddened. "Aw, that's nice of ya to say, especially 'cause I don't talk very good. I'm glad ya got what I was sayin.' I'm a little self-conscious."

"You're from Brooklyn."

"Mount Vernon. But my dad was from Brooklyn, which isn't that far away. His accent kinda rubbed off on me. I'm tryin' to get better, but after twenty years of droppin' my *G*s, it ain't—*it isn't*—easy."

"Don't change yourself. There's something about a Brooklyn accent that sounds honest."

"Most people say it sounds ugly."

"Tell them to stuff a sock in it."

"Yeah," she chortled. "That's what I do."

She stood. "Well, I guess I'd better get goin'. I take secretary classes at night. I'll just make it if I leave now." She tugged at the pocket of her uniform. "After all, I don't wanna work at Kress forever."

He was sorry to see her go. "Why don't you come again sometime?"

Her eyebrows lifted. "Ya want me to?"

"Sure. I like talking to you."

"Okay," she agreed. "How 'bout tomorrow?"

He grinned. "Sure, why not tomorrow?"

She gave him a cautious look. "But if Loretta's here when I come, I don't wanna get in the way."

His expression was doubtful. "There's not much chance of that. I don't expect her to come for at least a week, anyway."

"Okay, then, I'll see ya after work tomorrow." She started towards the door, then gasped and turned back. She snatched the paisley bag off the floor. "Will ya look at what I almost left behind!"

"Be careful with that," he cautioned.

She hugged the bag close to her chest. "I'm not lettin' it outta my sight." She waved goodbye as she left.

CHAPTER THIRTY-ONE

"Mrs. Truett, this is Doctor Leesburg."

Loretta sat on the sofa cradling the receiver beneath her chin. "Yes, Doctor." She closed her eyes. *Please don't give me bad news*, she thought. *My life is making sense. I can actually laugh again. Don't spoil it, please.*

"I'm calling to give you an update on your fiancé's condition. He's doing well. The bones in his legs are knitting. Nerve and muscle treatments are responding."

Loretta exhaled with relief without opening her eyes.

"We may be able to transfer him to plaster casts soon. As you know, he's scheduled for surgery on his lumbar region in a week. I assume you'll be here. I have other things to discuss with you regarding his rehabilitation."

She didn't open her eyes. "Are you telling me he'll recover?"

There was a pause. "I'm telling you he's improving."

She opened her eyes. "That's not a very good answer, Doctor. I need more than that."

His answer was terse. "We were able to save his legs, ma'am."

There was silence on both ends for several awkward seconds.

"Are you there?" Leesburg said.

"I'm here." She sank back against the couch cushions. "You can't tell me that with all your know-how, and all your education, and your great big hospital full of experts, that you can't do more to help Jack. I expect more."

When Leesburg answered, his tone bordered on hostility. "We're treating wards full of badly injured servicemen. More are arriving every day. All of them are young. All of them have families, and most of them had dreams they're never going to see happen. Each one of them is a hero, your fiancé included. You should know that more than anyone. You were out there with them.

"Can I assume you'll be here next week for the surgery, as he expects?"

She didn't answer.

"We'll be looking for you, Mrs. Truett. So will he."

Leesburg hung up.

Loretta poured a glass of wine.

***

She dreamed that night. She was on a beautiful beach with golden sand bordering aqua waters. The atmosphere was circus-like. Excited and high-spirited sailors, freed for a few hours from the rigors and dangers of their lives, cavorted like kids let loose on summer break.

Still high with joy from the lively USO show, they laughed, slapped backs, and milled around the entertainers who'd come down into the audience. Those men who emerged with autographs held them aloft like prize-winning trophies.

She stood with Drew Brackman, the fresh-faced boy with a shy smile, who'd somehow become Jack's best friend.

His eyes were lit from within with excitement and happiness. In a different setting, she could have envisioned him as a high school boy enjoying the neighborhood carnival. The only thing missing was a teenage girl on his arm.

Dorrie, she thought. *He'd be with Dorrie*.

That reminded her. She had something to give him.

"Is it all right if I return to the boat to retrieve something?" Loretta asked one of the Navy police standing close by." She looked at Drew. “Come on, Drew. This is for you. I want you to come with me.”

The crackle of a microphone split through the commotion. “Hear this! This is not a drill. Repeat, this is not a drill!”

“What are they talking about?” Loretta asked Drew with alarm.

“Something that shouldn’t be happening,” Drew gasped.

Then the planes appeared above them in the sky, distant at first, looking like black birds. They approached rapidly, more like hawks.

The planes whined as they plunged, their ammunition sounding like a buzz saw tearing through metal. Bullets hit the beach with heavy thuds, tearing up the sand.

Less than a foot away, an explosion of red splattered her as the MA, acting as her escort, jerked sideways like a puppet on a string.

She heard Drew’s cry behind her, felt his tackle.

Loretta awoke with a scream, her nightgown wet with sweat, her breathing labored and heavy.

She heard a frightened voice. “Mommy?”

She struggled to emerge from the nightmare that still clutched at her with inky black fingers. She gasped, trying to force herself back to full consciousness.

“Mommy?”

As the nightmare receded and the reality of her bedroom solidified, she was aware of her child, kneeling on the mattress beside her.

His face was terrified.

“Oh, baby!” she cried. She grabbed him into her arms and held him tight. “Oh, baby, it’s all right. Mommy just had a bad dream.” She rubbed his back and cooed soothingly into his hair. “Don’t be afraid. Mommy’s okay. It was just a dream.”

She pulled back and forced a smile to reassure him.

He wiped away the remaining tears on her face, his expression still frightened. “Did you have a monster under your bed?”

“No, honey, no. There are no monsters under beds. Mommy just had a bad dream, but it’s all gone now. Everything’s all right.”

Still shaking, she forced herself to react normally. She pulled back the covers and patted the place beside her. "Come on. Do you want to sleep with me the rest of the night?"

He snuggled into place beside her. "Are you going to have more bad dreams?" he asked cautiously.

"No more bad dreams," she assured him.

She made sure of it by not sleeping anymore that night.

Chapter Thirty-Two

The tension in the room was tangible. There wasn't a flicker of emotion on the granite faces. Not a twitch. There wasn't even the subtle curve of a lip or giveaway glint of an eye to betray the outcome.

Except for the methodical whir of a rotary fan in the warm room, there was only maddening silence.

The last play was critical. It could spell the difference between breaking a winning streak or going for broke. It was all or nothing.

"Got any fours?"

"Go fish."

Dorrie drew a card from the deck. "Ha!" She slapped her cards down on the bed. "I win again!" She leaned forward on her chair, smugly triumphant. "That's fifty toothpicks ya owe me." She shook her head. "Boy, if this is how ya played cards on the ship, I don't know how ya kept a bank account."

Astonished, Jack looked from his cards to her. "How do you keep *doing* that?"

"Doin' what?" She buffed her fingernails on the collar of her dress. "Beat the pants off-a ya every time we play cards, ya mean?"

"Yeah! I think you're cheating!"

"Well, I never." She scooped the cards off the bed and shuffled.

"What's a good Christian girl like you doing gambling, anyway?"

"Pretty good, I'd say. I don't wanna corrupt ya, but I don't think playin' with a friend for toothpicks is gamblin'." She thought for a moment, then gave him a stricken look. "Is it?"

He laughed at her honest dismay. "Only if the Treasury is switching gold for slivers of wood. As for corrupting me, you're way too late to take credit for that. I will tell you one thing, though, Dorrie the Greek, you'd better learn how to play fair or I'll call the cops. Worse yet, I'll call your pastor."

"Oh sure, tell me another." She shuffled the deck. "Ya wanna play again?"

"Losing five times in a row at Go Fish to a kid from Mount Vernon is more than my pride can take. Let's give it a rest."

Donovan poked her head into the room. "You two are having too much fun in here. Keep it down a little, okay?"

"Yes, ma'am," Dorrie said. She pointed at Jack. "It's his fault."

"It usually is," Donovan acknowledged.

"What do you mean, *my* fault!" Jack protested.

Donovan wagged a warning finger and ducked back out to return to her duties.

When she was gone, Dorrie said, "Wow, she's tough."

"Aah," Jack scoffed. "I can handle her."

Dorrie put the cards back in the pack. "Hey, tell me somethin'. Did the prayer for your back work?"

"I forgot about that," he said. "I don't know." He shifted slightly as if to test, then winced at the twinges of pain up his back and legs. "I wouldn't say I feel great, but I don't feel like climbing the walls, either. I think I'm just getting used to less morphine."

"Hey. Give credit where it's due. Ya wanna talk any more about Drew's Bible?"

He cocked an eyebrow. "If I didn't know better, I'd think you're trying to convert me, girl."

"Nah," she said. "Convertin's somethin' ya do when you're tryin' to get somebody to like your religion. I'm just tellin' ya about Jesus."

"Oh," he said with mock insight. "Because Jesus isn't a religion, he's a person."

"See? I taught ya well," She hesitated, then said, "Did ya notice I said well and not good?"

He grinned. "Congratulations. But don't let them teach you too much. Don't lose that accent."

"Oh, the sooner I get rid of it, the better off I'll be." She tucked the cards into her purse. "When's the surgery on your back? Have they moved it up any?"

"Shouldn't be long now."

"Loretta will be here for that, right?"

"Who knows?" he shrugged. "She just got handed a contract."

Dorrie heaved a sigh. "I wanna say somethin', but I'm afraid you'll get mad at me."

"I couldn't get mad at you."

"Ya might in just a second. I was thinkin' it's too bad Loretta can't be with ya more often. It would make it a lot easier for ya. Has she even been here more than that one time?"

Jack made a gesture of dismissal. "Nothing she can do except sit around and watch me get thinner. I don't blame her. She's got a career to think about. Besides, it's better if we just get to know each other again when all this is over and I'm out of here. I mean, when I can walk again, you know."

"That sounds right," Dorrie said.

She surprised him. "You're the first person who hasn't tried to set me straight about that."

"Well, never say never, I always say. Anyway, there's somebody better to ask about that than me."

He was annoyed. "For once, Dorrie, can't you just answer a straight question without talking about God?"

"Probably not," she shrugged, unfazed. "Somethin' you'll just have to get used to. Ya want me to tell ya about the future, but I can't do that. All I can tell ya is what I believe."

He scowled. "All right. You keep telling me about this God of yours who let Drew get killed and landed me here. Was Drew getting killed the answer to your prayers?"

He immediately regretted his outburst, but he couldn't take it back, and he honestly wanted her answer.

She frowned and looked down at her hands in her lap. When she looked up again, her eyes were grieved. "I don't know why God let Drew die. I love Drew with all my heart, and I always will. But I know who I can trust, too, and I'll tell ya why."

She sank back in the chair. "Jesus got beat up so bad that he didn't look like a human person anymore. They spit on him and pulled his beard out with their hands. Then they hammered great big spikes through his hands and feet. And he could have stopped it at any second, but he didn't. Know why?"

Jack was silent, afraid he'd snap if he spoke.

"Because," she said, "He knew that what he was doin' was gonna be better for everybody in the long run. That's somebody I can trust. I don't know if any of this makes sense to ya, but did ya ever think about this? If Drew hadn't been out there with Loretta at just that second, she'd be dead now.

"I don't know if that's the reason God took Drew, but I have to trust Jesus because he suffered so much himself. He knows what he's doin', even if I don't."

She pulled a hanky from her pocket and dabbed her eyes. "Look at me, cryin' like a dope. I didn't mean to start bawlin'."

Jack grimaced, ashamed of himself. "I'm sorry."

She shook her head. "Ya don't have to say that. You're hurtin' and you're tryin' to figure things out, I know that." She reached over and patted his hand. "There's somethin' ya don't understand 'cause you don't know. Jesus reaches me." She laid her hand across her heart. "In here. That's why I can trust him. I know he's there.

"Don't go beatin' yourself up when I leave here today. It's okay, I know how ya feel." She stood. "Listen, I know this is kinda bad timin' after all the things we just said, but I gotta leave or I'll be late for class. We've got finals comin' up, so I'll be crammin' for a few days."

I've messed up again, he thought. *I've just pushed away the only friend I have right now.*

"I'll be back the day ya have your surgery," Dorrie said. "I'll call the hospital to make sure I got the right day. If Loretta's here, I'll make myself scarce. But I'll come to check, just in case."

She leaned down and kissed his cheek. "Maybe next time I should bring Rook instead of Go Fish. Ya might be better at that."

Relief swelled inside him. "Sure, I've got to win back my toothpicks."

She grinned and wiped the last of the tears from her face with the back of her hand. "I'll see ya later, honey."

Chapter Thirty-Three

Loretta was distant and distracted on the set the next day, flubbing lines and missing important cues. When her scenes were over, she excused herself to a private nook where she could be alone.

Meadows drove Loretta home from the studio that evening, then sat with her in the driveway behind the privacy gates.

"You're not yourself today," he said, switching off the car engine. "And before you tell me that there's nothing wrong, I know there is."

Wrapped up in her thoughts, she barely heard him. When his words registered, she tsked lightly and waved away his concern. "It's nothing. No reason to worry. I'm just having an off day."

"I see." He was silent for a moment, then gave her a knowing look. "If you'll allow me to make an observation, you've been a complete professional from the day you first stepped foot on that soundstage. Everyone, from the script girl to Morris Samuels, finds you impressive. But today, you acted just like a girl in a high school play trying to remember her lines."

He held a hand up against the righteous indignation that flashed in her eyes. "Don't waste time protesting. Just tell me what's troubling you."

She briefly considered opening the car door and telling him goodnight, but she had no one else to talk to. "It's Jack."

"Of course," he sighed. "It's always Jack."

"He's having surgery on Friday, and his doctors want me to be there."

Meadows shrugged. "Why? So they can remind you that he doesn't have a chance of ever living a normal life again, and neither will you?"

She wanted to be angry, but couldn't deny what he was saying.

"Or maybe it's so you can smile and laugh and assure him of your undying devotion," he went on, "when you know that all you feel is dread."

She felt invaded hearing him say out loud what she was privately thinking. "How can you say an awful thing like that?" she whispered. "Jack could never be any trouble to me, even if he was hurt ten times worse than he is now. If you only knew him. If you only knew what a good man he is, and how brave he's been."

Meadows nodded. "I'm sure he's good, and I know he's brave. I'm sure you love him, and he loves you even more. But my dear Loretta, have you ever asked yourself whether you're the right person for him at this time?"

Her eyes flashed. "Don't say that!"

He sighed. "I'm honest. It always gets me into trouble. I'm going to risk getting into more right now by telling you that Jack's demands on you are going to start requiring more than you'll be willing to give." He held up a hand. "Don't interrupt me. Let me finish."

He waited for her response. When he received none, he continued. "Right now, he's in the hands of professionals who look after his every need and keep a close eye on him in case something goes wrong. It's a full-time job and takes a team of experts."

"That's why I've taken these roles. I'm hiring a medical team to help him."

"And how will he feel knowing that he depends on you for that?"

"Frank, you just don't understand!"

"I understand that you knew him before the war, when life was different." He raised his eyebrows. "Can you honestly tell me that Jack is still the same person you kissed goodbye?"

She lowered her head. "It's not just that. His friend saved my life."

Frank nodded. "I see. So then, you'll not only be serving Jack out of a sense of obligation, but guilt, too."

She looked up. "I'm having nightmares. I see things now I didn't before."

"Ah," Frank said. "I wondered when that might begin to happen."

"How can I tell Jack that every time I look at him, I'll have to relive that horrible experience again? How can I tell him I still love him, but that I don't want to see him again? Oh, Frank! It's not my career that's keeping me from him." Tears flooded her eyes. "It's that he reminds me! When I think of him, even now, all I see is that beach!"

To his surprise, she wrapped her arms around his neck and cried. He let her cry for a long time.

He raised his eyebrows. This was happening faster than he'd expected. He suppressed a smile. "Go on, darling. I'm here."

Chapter Thirty-Four

Like the worship centers on many Navy vessels, the San Diego base chapel was plain. There were rows of wooden benches, a few hymnals, and Bibles in racks on the back of each pew. Up front, American and Navy flags flanked a rough-hewn pulpit and suspended cross.

With rain falling and the midweek slow, Smitty figured he'd have the chapel to himself.

After duty, instead of going into town, he donned a regulation black oilskin slicker, stuffed the letter he'd gotten from Jack that morning in his pocket, and headed to the chapel.

The place was quiet, as he'd suspected it would be. The red, gold, and blue stained-glass windows, usually so vibrant in the sun, were muted by the hour and weather, their colorful images flat.

Smitty didn't remove his rain-splattered slicker as he entered and sat in the last pew near the door. He wanted to be ready to make a hasty retreat in case anyone came in.

He appreciated the solitude, but the silence was dangerous. It let the images and voices creep in, memories he fought to bury. Daylight, laughter, and the hum of duty helped keep them at bay. Sometimes, he almost felt normal. But tonight, the rain and the dark pulled him into the void again.

The chapel seemed more inviting than another pointless evening in town, especially after reading what Jack had written in the letter Smitty had received that morning.

He withdrew the soggy sheets from his slicker pocket and read for the tenth time that day:

Hey, Smit. It's been a while since I got your letter. Sorry, it's taken me so long to get back. I've been busy patching up here.

About those medals you won. You deserve 'em. You saved Loretta's life. In my book, that's worth the Medal of Honor. Too bad I'm not the one who makes those decisions.

I don't hear anybody in the newspapers talking about what you did, but I want you to know, for what it's worth, that I know. You saved my worthless hide, too— twice, if I'm counting right. Gotta admit, that still makes me scratch my head. I was pretty sure you were cooking up ways to kill me on the ship instead of ways to keep me alive.

Also glad to hear you're thinking about what Brackman said about the ticket. I have been, too. In fact, Drew's girl, Dorrie, has been coming up every few days to keep me company while Loretta's busy. She's been explaining things to me.

Smart Kid, a real character. Too bad Brackman's not here to back her up, but what Dorrie has been telling me is starting to make sense. I don't think I'll be singing in the choir anytime soon, but who knows? Like Dorrie says, never say never.

Don't know what else to tell you about what's happening with me. The doctor says I'm in bad shape. He says I probably won't ever walk again, but I don't put much stock in white coats. I say it's mind over matter.

Loretta's doing swell. She just got a movie contract. I guess moving to California is on the horizon for us. I'll look you up when we get there, and we'll lift a mug.

That's it for now. Write again if you feel up to it.

Jack

Smitty stuffed the letter back in his pocket. For several minutes, he sat still, staring ahead, trying to discipline his thoughts and find a little peace before heading back to the barracks to face the dreaded task of falling asleep.

It wasn't working. A groan escaped him as he dropped his head, fingers gripping his rain-damp hair. "Help me," he choked out. His shoulders shook. "Please, God. Please help me." He rocked forward, putting his forehead on the top of the pew ahead. He gripped the wood tightly with both hands until his fingers turned white.

Consumed in his desperate plea, he didn't hear the approach of the chaplain, who'd arrived to lock up for the night.

Chapter Thirty-Five

Loretta's telegram came on the day of his surgery.

FORCED TO REMAIN HERE STOP SHOOTING SCHEDULE CHANGED STOP GOOD LUCK STOP MUST DISCUSS FUTURE STOP

It was over. Numb with disappointment and grief, Jack let the telegram slip out of his fingers onto the floor.

Good luck, she'd said. She hadn't signed with her love. She could have been writing to a stranger. He knew what she wanted to discuss about the future.

I was fooling myself, he thought. *She's got a life. She's got a career. I've been unfair. I should have cut her loose the first day. I've been a selfish jerk, thinking this would work. I should have given her a break right from the beginning.*

Donovan came in to check his vitals and saw the telegram on the floor. She stooped to retrieve it.

"Read it," Jack said evenly.

She gave him a curious look. After reading, she looked at him with a pained expression. "Jack, I don't know what to say. I'm so sorry."

He swallowed hard. "Would you bring me something to write with? I need to write her a letter."

Donovan left and returned a few minutes later. "Don't do anything rash." She handed him the paper and pen. "It might not be as bad as it looks. Telegrams can be so terse."

"It's okay," he said. "I know how it is."

She quickly checked his vitals and left.

Dear Loretta. Jack wrote. *I got your telegram. I'm going into surgery in a few hours, and I wanted to write this before they knock me out.*

Honey, you know you mean the world to me. It's because I care that I'm cutting you loose. I'm not fooling myself anymore, and I don't want you to, either. I don't know what's going to happen, but one thing I know for sure is that I'll feel like a third wheel if we stay together.

I'm not blaming you. God knows I'm not. I don't mean it to sound that way. A good friend told me that God has a way of knowing what's best for us. I think this is the best for us. I've still got my pride. I'd like to keep it.

I think it's best if you don't contact me. Please respect my wishes. Break a leg, Baby.

Love – Jack

P.S. I'm sending Rusty my Silver Star and Purple Heart. I promised him medals. Let him brag and show them around his class for a while. As he gets older, he'll find new heroes, but for now, let him enjoy them. If you have a way to find me in the future, you can send them back to me when he's outgrown them.

He finished writing the letter. He tore it from the notepad, folded it, and waited for one of his nurses to come in.

It was Donovan. He handed her the folded page. "Send that to Loretta for me, will you?"

She nodded and turned to leave, but he called her back. "Send her both of my medals, but keep the award letters for me."

She opened her mouth to argue.

"It's okay," he assured her. "They're for her son Rusty. He's a great kid."

She nodded. "I'll send it out right away."

He lay thinking about what life with Loretta could have been. He wondered if there'd been any way he could have avoided the accident. Had the gun that crushed him been one of those he'd been working on before the attack? If so, did he cause his own injury? Was he the cause of all this?

After an hour of reflection, he prayed. *God, I've been listening to the things Dorrie's been telling me about you. I've got to be honest, I'm confused. But I've been lying here doing a lot of thinking.*

Drew and Dorrie are the only two straight shooters I've ever met. I trust what they told me. From what I hear, you went to a lot of trouble to make it square for everybody. I don't know what that means, exactly, but I think I've got an idea. I'm willing to take the chance that you know what's best.

My life hasn't been squeaky clean, and I'm sorry about that. I always thought I was doing things the right way. But if you want me, Jesus, you've got me, and I'll let you handle the rest. I'll stop doing things my way and hitch in your direction, like Drew said, if you'll show me how.

Give me a ticket to the show. I want in. Thanks a lot. Drew and Dorrie always stopped praying by saying, 'In Jesus' name,' so that's how I'll end this.

He sighed and opened his eyes. "Well, that's it," he said aloud. "What now? Am I supposed to hear angels or something?" Dorrie said that really believing, not just saying words, was important. He thought carefully. After all he'd learned, he *knew* he believed.

The medical staff, including Donovan, came in to prep him for surgery.

"Wait a second," he said as they wheeled him from the room, the traction apparatus still intact. "I need to leave a note for someone in case I'm out for a while. She might be coming today."

"Better hurry," one orderly said. "They're waiting for you."

Donovan pulled a pencil and a scrap of yellow paper from her apron. "I've learned to keep paper handy when I'm near you, sailor! Sorry, this is all I have."

"It'll do," he assured her.

He jotted: *Took the ticket—talk to you later*—and handed it to Donovan. "Dorrie's probably going to come today. Give that to her, will ya?"

Donovan nodded. "I'll be sure she gets it."

"Okay. Wish me luck. No wait!" He grinned mischievously. "Say a prayer for me. I think that's what I'm supposed to say if I've got the lingo right."

"Good luck, sailor," Donovan said. "You'll come through fine."

Chapter Thirty-Six

Dorrie burst through the double doors of the hospital, skidding to a stop outside Jack's empty room.

"I wish someone would tell that girl that this is a hospital and not the training ground for the Olympic running team," one nurse grumbled to another.

"Where is he?" Dorrie demanded of a passing orderly. "Is he in surgery already? Am I late?"

The orderly looked at his watch. "Fifteen minutes now."

"Is Loretta here?"

Donovan waved the orderly on. "I'll take care of it, thanks."

"Is Loretta here?" Dorrie repeated.

"No, honey, she's not here," Donovan said.

"Whattya mean she's not here? Ya mean to tell me she wasn't sittin' there beside Jack's bed?" She attempted to calm herself. "Well, then, she's probably just late like I was, that's all."

"No, she's just not coming."

Dorrie's eyes narrowed.

"If you want to sit here in the hallway until he comes out of surgery, you can," Donovan said. "It's up to you, but he'll be in there for a few hours, then he'll be asleep. Why don't you go home and come back tomorrow? He'll be awake then."

Dorrie pressed her lips and shook her head. "I'm not goin' anywhere. If Loretta's not comin', then I'm gonna play backup. You just show me where the bathrooms are and I'll wait."

"Okay, have it your own—" She paused. "Oh, wait, I nearly forgot." She dug in her pocket. "He thought you might be here, so he asked me to give you this note."

She handed the yellow slip to Dorrie.

Dorrie's eyes widened as she read. She dropped the note and slapped both hands across her mouth.

Donovan could tell she was about to shout. "Don't yell!"

Dorrie stared at her, eyes still wide, hands still across her mouth. Slowly, she lowered her hands. "He took the ticket," she breathed. "Thank you, Jesus, he took the ticket!"

Donovan patted her shoulder. "Well, whatever that means, I'm happy for both of you." She grinned, motioned to a chair outside Jack's room, and said, "You can sit there."

Dorrie scooped the slip of paper from the floor and tucked it into her dress pocket.

For two hours, she sat patiently, waiting and praying. When the third hour rolled around, she grabbed Donovan's arm as she walked by. "It's takin' longer than ya said it would."

"Sometimes they just need a little more time," Donovan assured her.

"What're they doin' now?" Dorrie asked. "He's sleepin', right?"

"He's sleeping, and he doesn't feel a thing. Don't worry so much. He's going to be better coming out than he was going in."

Another hour passed. She thought about Drew, wishing he'd had the chance Jack was getting.

She sighed and leaned back. It was hard to get comfortable in a stiff chair after sitting for hours.

As hour five elapsed, the doors to the floor opened, and a gurney was wheeled through.

Dorrie glanced up with only cursory interest. There had been several patients through that door throughout the day. She didn't expect this one to be Jack any more than any of the others had.

But it was.

She shot to her feet. "Jack!"

The attendant taking Jack to his room hesitated long enough for her to peer down into his sleeping face.

"He's just asleep," he assured her.

Dorrie trailed behind as they wheeled him to the room. Visiting hours were almost over, and she wasn't sure they'd allow her to stay. One thing she knew for sure. If they wouldn't let her stay on the floor or in his room, she'd sit in the lobby until he woke up, even if it took days. He needed Loretta, but if she couldn't come, then he needed a friend.

As Donovan left for the evening, she walked through the lobby. There, she spotted Dorrie sitting in a hard chair.

Donovan sat beside her. "You planning to sleep here?"

Dorrie nodded.

"May I make a suggestion?"

Dorrie nodded again.

"Why don't you go home? Come back in the morning when you're nice and refreshed. Jack's going to sleep all night. He won't even know you're here."

"You sure?" Dorrie asked uncertainly.

"Positive," Donovan said.

***

Jack awakened near dawn, feeling like a fleet of Navy convoys had run him over. His head felt like it had been packed with grenades that went off every time he drew a breath. Why weren't the painkillers working? He had bad news for Leesburg if this surgery was supposed to improve the quality of his life.

By the time the clock read seven a.m., life felt better. Leesburg took a seat beside his bed. "You look almost human again."

Jack groaned. "I wish I felt that way. I think I felt better when the cannon fell on me."

"You'll feel better in a few hours," Leesburg said. "We'll talk later about what you can expect from now on. For one thing, you should be discharged to rehabilitation in about six weeks. I couldn't reach your fiancée. She told me she plans to hire a nurse to help you at home during your transition."

Jack grimaced. "Doc, I don't have a fiancée anymore. Loretta and I—well, it's over between us."

Leesburg wasn't surprised. "Very unfortunate."

"Happens."

"That creates a few problems," Leesburg said. "Do you have other friends who can help you while you're recovering? I know you have no living relatives."

"No."

"You'll need help. When your fiancée and I spoke, I tried to convince her that your best option would be to use a Navy rehabilitation center. After that, once you're home, you'll still need assistance, but you'll be more functional.

"In a way, this works out better for you. Your fiancée wasn't thinking logically. Once you're through therapy, they'll assign a social worker to offer suggestions."

"I can take care of him when he's ready to come home," a quiet voice said.

Leesburg swiveled in his chair to see Dorrie standing in the doorway. She walked past Leesburg as though he weren't there and stood beside Jack's bed. "Are ya sayin' that you and Loretta called it off?" she asked. "Is that what you're sayin'?"

Jack nodded.

Dorrie turned to Leesburg. "I'm sorry. I didn't mean to listen, but I can take care of Jack when he comes home if he needs it and doesn't have anybody else."

Jack thought of a few responses he could have had: indignation, embarrassment, stubborn pride. Instead, he felt a rush of warmth. "Dorrie, listen. This is serious. It's not something for a kid like you to take on."

She straightened. "Don't you call me a kid."

"If you're thinking about doing this for Drew—"

Leesburg stood. "I'll leave the two of you to discuss it. I'll send a social worker in sometime this week to give you some ideas."

"Thanks, Doc," Jack said.

When he was gone, Dorrie sat in her usual place beside Jack's bed. "I don't mean to yell at ya, but ya need to get this straight. I'm not offerin' to help because of Drew. You're my friend. If I can help, then I wanna. And it's not 'cause I owe it to anybody." She paused, eyebrows rising. "But before I say anything else, I just can't stand the suspense. I gotta ask. Did ya really take the ticket?"

He nodded. "Right before I went into surgery." He hesitated. "I meant it. At least, I hope I did."

She gave him a curious look.

"If I'm being honest," he said. "I might have done it because I need something solid in my life right now." He shook his head, frustrated. "I mean, my legs don't work, I don't have a career, Loretta's gone. I even got kicked out of the Navy. You said I have to believe it like it's real. Not like it's a religion. That's what Drew said. That's what you said."

She nodded.

He weighed his next words carefully. He'd never been one to explain his feelings or even admit that he had any. But Dorrie was safe. He knew he could trust her.

"I don't want one more fake relationship. If this is real, I've got to know for sure that I'm not just falling back on it until something else comes along." His look asked her to understand. "I need to know that even if I get my legs back, I'm not gonna forget God the way Loretta forgot me."

"I can't believe she did that. Doesn't sound like the girl I met."

"Don't feel sorry for me," Jack smirked. "If it had been Loretta who landed here instead of me, I would've been the one to take a powder, and I probably would have done it a lot sooner. Especially if someone offered me a new gig on stage."

"I don't believe that."

"Believe it. I'm not the nice guy you think I am." He was quiet for a moment. "Drew showed me a different way, though. He didn't act like everybody else. He had a big heart, but he wasn't a chicken." He smiled at a memory. "We were talking about dames once—you'll pardon the expression. He was giving me a hard time for foolin' around even though I was engaged. He said, I don't need anybody but Dorrie. She's girl enough for me."

Dorrie gasped and dropped her face into her hands.

Jack grimaced. "I shouldn't have told you that. I'm always saying the wrong thing."

She looked up teary-eyed, but grinning. "Join the club! I'm so glad ya told me! Ya don't know how much that means to me! It's like he just gave me a great big hug!"

Jack gave a small grin, relieved.

She bent forward to kiss his cheek. "Well, you've got a friend here. And if ya want to find out if what you've got with God is real, I'll go along with ya if ya want me to."

He hesitated. He didn't want to insult her, but he knew he couldn't take advantage of her, either. "You've been terrific. But you're a single girl, and you're young. You'll find somebody someday, and I don't want to saddle you."

"So, what're ya sayin'? You think I'm gonna run out on ya?"

"I'm saying you've got a life. You'll meet a guy someday who's head over heels for you. He might not want a guy in a wheelchair taking up your time."

"Well, I believe that whatever happens is supposed to happen if ya belong to Jesus. So why don't we just take it day-by-day and stop tryin' to figure it all out in advance? I'm not gonna run out on ya, but if somethin' ever happened, God would give ya all the help ya need to get through. Besides, maybe you're the one who'd get married instead of me."

He snorted. "Sure. Like anybody's gonna give me a second look these days."

She was shocked. "Are you kiddin'? You've got a face that makes girls look twice!"

"And a wheelchair that makes 'em run the other way."

"Tell me, somethin'," she sighed. "Have ya always been such a yutz?"

He looked puzzled. "That depends. What's a yutz?"

"It's Jewish for dummy. My landlady taught me that."

"Oh. Then, yeah, I've always been a yutz."

She sniffed. "Tell me somethin' I don't know."

Chapter Thirty-Seven

The morning the package arrived, Loretta was waiting for Frank to drive her to the set. They were nearing completion on *The Burden of the Day*, and sets were already being constructed for *Art Déco.*

The guard in the security booth near her circular driveway walked to her door and laid the brown package on the step. He rang the doorbell and returned to his post.

Loretta recognized the hospital address immediately, even without picking the package up. She stared at it with dread.

The security gate opened, and Frank's car came through.

Loretta nudged the package with her shoe into the foyer. She hoped to forget about it until she got home that evening.

"Russell, I'm leaving," she called. "Your nanny will be here in five minutes. Please don't get into anything until she comes!"

Quickly shutting the door, she skipped down the stairs to meet her co-star. She was becoming a good actress. She gave him a bright, cheerful wave and jumped into the seat of the expensive car with a cheery, "Good morning!"

"Well," Frank approved. "You're chipper today! You usually don't look this alive until at least ten a.m."

"I'm just looking forward to seeing the movie finished," she smiled brightly. "After all, I've never seen myself on a movie screen before. Let's get this one finished so we can start on the next!"

She kept up a cheerful front all day. By the end, she nearly believed it herself. She even almost endeared herself to Marinell by laughing at her terrible jokes.

Loretta normally preferred to be home before Russell went to bed, but she stayed out late that night. She and Frank laughed and drank too much before she realized she'd run out of time and places to hide.

"Come on, let's get you home," Frank said. "It's late. May I stay?"

She laid a hand on his chest. "Not tonight, Frank. I've had such a full day, I think I'm just going to go home and collapse into a coma, all by myself."

He sighed, disappointed. "I'll try not to be too bothered. Well, I'll drive you home at least."

She reluctantly accepted. She wasn't sure where their relationship was headed, but she had already crossed lines with him that she hadn't given Jack until their romance was more mature.

In many ways, Frank reminded her of Moe Truett—older, more experienced, richer. But Frank was more sincere. Moe had used her to satisfy his ego. It seemed Frank genuinely cared. With all the drama in her life lately, she didn't know how she'd have managed without him.

She maintained a carefree facade when he dropped her at the door, kissed him, and waved goodnight.

She hated going inside.

Russell's nanny, Anna, met her at the door when she arrived. "Good evening, Miss," she said. Her tone was tired and terse.

"Oh, Anna, good evening! I'm so sorry. I didn't call to let you know I'd be home late this evening, did I?"

"No, you didn't, Miss. But it's not evening anymore. It's one o'clock in the morning."

Loretta made an appropriately apologetic face. "I won't be working tomorrow, so please take the day off with pay. I'm so very sorry. The day just got away."

Anna felt slightly mollified. "It's all right, Miss. I put Russell to bed at eight o'clock." She collected her purse from the long coffee table near the door, where it sat next to the package from the hospital. "This package was on the floor when I came this morning," she said, pointing to it.

Loretta nodded. "Thanks, Anna. I'll see you the day after tomorrow."

"Good night, Miss."

When she was gone, Loretta stood staring at the package. Finally, she found the courage to pick it up. She sat on the sofa, wishing she had a glass of wine, but knowing she'd had too much already this evening.

She laid the package on her lap, unwrapped the string, and tore the brown paper away. There was a sheet of yellow paper folded around two oblong blue boxes. She unfolded the paper and read Jack's letter.

She'd known he would respond. She hadn't known how, but this was not what she'd expected.

At the hospital, she couldn't tell him he wouldn't walk again. But staying away while he suffered felt like a bigger betrayal.

She hadn't known how to explain that seeing him, even thinking about him, only reawakened the nightmare of Azure Verde. How could he understand? She realized only now that for two years, he'd lived almost every day what she'd experienced for a few terrifying minutes.

The weight of his decision crashed down on her. "Oh, Jack—" With trembling hands, she opened the first box. The glittering five-pointed Silver Star glinted at her from its gold-plated base. She turned the medal over and read the words: F*or Gallantry in Action.* Choking, she opened the second box. The Purple Heart, for being wounded in battle.

Loretta clutched the boxes against her chest. Her hair fell forward, curtaining her face.

"Jack," she whispered. "I didn't mean for it to happen this way. I'm sorry. It's my fault."

"Mommy," Russell said from the door of his bedroom. He'd seen her crying too often lately, but he knew how to comfort her now.

Loretta wiped tears from her face. "What are you doing up so late, Admiral?"

He climbed up on the sofa beside her and put his small arms around her. "Don't cry, Mommy. I'll take care of you."

She choked back tears and hugged him tight, then she pulled away from him. "I have something to show you."

She opened the Silver Star box and handed it to him.

Russell's eyes grew large. He sucked in his breath. She'd never known him to be so still. For at least a minute, he stared at the medal, his breath coming in quick gasps. Finally, he turned his wondering gaze on her. "Is it Uncle Jack's medal?" he whispered in awe.

Loretta sniffled and nodded. "It's the Silver Star, an important medal. It means Uncle Jack was very brave."

"Wow," Russell breathed. He ran his fingers across the star in the center. "Wow, Uncle Jack's medal."

Loretta handed him the second box. "Here's another one. This is the Purple Heart. Uncle Jack got this for being wounded in battle."

"Because he broke his arm?" Russell breathed reverently.

Loretta nodded.

"Wow," Russell said again.

They sat together on the sofa for fifteen minutes. Russell didn't speak.

"You can show them at school tomorrow if you're careful with them," Loretta said. "But then they have to go into the safe."

"Can I look at them sometimes?" Russell asked.

She nodded.

He clasped the closed boxes against his chest. "Can I sleep with them tonight?"

She hugged him. "Of course you can, darling."

Chapter Thirty-Eight

At lunchtime, Donovan and Atilla heard the Paul Campor radio broadcast.

Hold onto your hats, ladies and gentlemen, hold onto your hats. The Loretta Truett and Brian Jackson story just took a twist that your Stay Tuned correspondent never saw coming. Truth is stranger than fiction, they say.

"You can say that again," Atilla muttered. "Never had a patient like this one before, with a movie star for a girlfriend."

"Let's hear this," Donovan shushed.

While you enjoy watching Loretta in her brand-new movie, The Burden of the Day with Franklin Meadows, she's facing heartache on a grand scale back home. Scuttlebutt has it that it's quits between Loretta and her war hero fiancé, Brian Jackson.

"Is that right?" Atilla said, surprised.

Donovan frowned. "Truett must have spilled the beans."

As everyone in America knows, Gunner's Mate Jackson was injured in the battle that nearly killed Loretta in the Pacific. It's the stuff of fairy tales, listeners. The gallant cavalier who risked his life for the woman he loves has spent the last few months in the hospital, but word has it that the prognosis is bleak.

"Where are they getting this?" Atilla protested. "That kind of information is privileged."

Donovan thought about Loretta's telegram to Jack. Any sympathy she might have had for the woman evaporated.

Campor continued. *And get this, according to Samuels Brothers Studios, Jackson has pleaded with Loretta to let him go.*

Donovan dropped her face into her hands and shook her head. "I can't believe I'm hearing this bull."

Now, to respect his wishes, Loretta must find a way to live without him. Rumor has it that she was offered another upcoming movie role with Franklin Meadows called Art Deco. She was ready to say no, but Jackson insisted she take the role and follow her path.

This is the definition of courage, Stay Tuned listeners. Think of Loretta Truett with love and admiration as you see her now in The Burden of the Day, and give her your support in Art Deco when it's released next year.

This is your Stay Tuned correspondent, Paul Campor, signing off.

Donovan savagely flicked off the radio dial and shot to her feet. "Excuse me. I'm feeling sick."

Chapter Thirty-Nine

It took only days after the Paul Campor *Stay Tuned* broadcast for the press to leave.

Jack's transfer to a rehabilitation facility happened five weeks later.

The first week was a blur of assessments, schedules, and learning what his new reality would be.

"Think of these as your new best friends," David, his reconstruction aide, said as he handed him a pair of transfer boards. David was in his fifties but still had the frame of a bodybuilder. "These'll help you transfer from bed to chair, chair to toilet, things like that. Independence starts with movement."

The transfers were harder at first than Jack had imagined, especially with his back still healing. His shoulders and arms quivered and burned as he lifted his full body weight, sliding from surface to surface.

David was patient but firm. "Your back muscles are stronger than you think. Don't be afraid to use them."

Within a month, Jack could dress himself, though getting his legs into pants still required careful maneuvering and time.

The therapist taught him to massage his legs, check for pressure sores, and maintain circulation in his muscles.

"Your legs are still part of you. Take care of them and they won't cause you problems."

Dorrie came every day after work, often with the pastor and other members of the church. She'd arrive just as Jack was finishing his exercises, soaked in sweat and frustrated.

"Don't give up," she encouraged. "You'll get it."

Bible studies and talks with the pastor, Dorrie, and the others made him eager to know more. He understood now what Drew and Dorrie had meant about God's presence inside. If he'd been asked to define it, he couldn't have. He just knew it was there, and it was a warmth and reassurance he'd never felt before.

He regretted not understanding sooner and not being able to tell Drew about it.

"Oh, don't worry," Dorrie said. "You'll get the chance to tell him someday."

He wasn't sure where his relationship with Dorrie was headed or if it was already in the most perfect place. As much as he loved her, Dorrie was Drew's girl. For another, romance had a bad habit of wrecking friendships.

It was an issue for another time. For now, learning how to function on his own was most important. He was determined not to saddle Dorrie or anyone else with his problems.

Water therapy became the highlight of his week. The pool was small, but most rehab facilities had none, so he was grateful for it. In the pool, supported by the water, he could move almost normally. The first time he swam a few strokes using only his arms, Dorrie cheered from the side of the pool.

"Show off!" she called.

He splashed her. She ran around the pool's edge to avoid him, her shoes squeaking on the wet tiles, while he pursued her as best he could through the water. For those moments, the wheelchair sitting empty at the pool's edge might as well not have existed.

Donovan came often, too. She shared meals, patiently endured their talks about God, and promised to visit the church someday.

"Do it, Donnie," Jack urged. He told her about the ticket.

After several weeks of therapy, the final prognosis came down. Jack wouldn't walk again. The glimmer of hope they'd given him at the hospital was gone, but he was less disappointed than he thought he'd be. He hadn't expected a good report, but his body was stronger now, and he was more capable. He could transfer himself faster than some orderlies could help him, and his shoulders and chest had broadened from constant use.

On the morning of his fifth month at the facility, newly accommodated with a fifty-pound wheelchair he'd learned to maneuver, and leg braces to prevent muscle contractions, he was discharged home.

The church arranged for him to use a cottage near the sanctuary.

The library and the YMCA were just a block and a half away. Volunteers from both places stood ready to help him with the curbs and traffic. A grocer along the way made shopping easier.

Jack knew how drastically his life had changed in a year, but he was grateful for how much he could still do. After only a short time at home, he was back on course.

A few major hurdles persisted, though. The daily newspaper and radio broadcasts with news of the war made him feel like a slacker. He yearned to be back out there, doing his part.

Drew, Unger, Peterson, Widdon, and others— all the comrades he'd known and outlived— were an involuntary part of his daily reflections.

His second large challenge was the movie theater along his daily route. He avoided looking at the marquee whenever he passed.

Chapter Forty

In December, Michie Stadium at West Point hosted the Army-Navy football game, limiting attendance to fifteen thousand fans. Because of the war, officials canceled most pro and amateur sports, but the Army-Navy game, played by cadets, was still on.

The weather was cold with a chance of snow, but no one complained. Bundled, huddled, and enthusiastic, cold weather was no deterrent.

The outing was Jack's first significant venture since coming home. Almost the whole church was there. They found a spot on the first level where his wheelchair could sit beside the bleachers without blocking foot traffic. The spot blended well and didn't stick out like a sore thumb, which made him feel less like a sideshow.

Dorrie plunked herself firmly beside him. "Hey, there, Navy, let's beat Army!"

She pointed at the field where the players were setting up. "Wow, look at those guys. Don't they look great? I like the way guys look in football uniforms."

"I thought you said you liked the way guys look in Navy uniforms."

"They both work." She rubbed her gloved hands together, put her arm through Jack's, and huddled closer to stay warm.

In the first quarter, the Navy came out strong and never let up.

Jack hadn't missed his freedom of movement as much as now. Navy was crushing Army, but he believed they would perform even better if he could stand, raise his fist, and cheer them on.

After one bad Navy pass, though, he threw his arms up and yelled, "Hey! What the—! You call yourself a quarterback! My great-grandmother in bedroom slippers could've made a better pass! You call yourself a Navy man? Get somebody to teach you how to Paaaaaasssss!"

Dorrie was about to comment on his lack of good Christian manners when another play went wrong. She leaped to her feet, grabbed the railing, and leaned so far over that Jack was worried she'd tumble over. "Hey!" she shrieked. "He was wide open on the five-yard line! What's the matter with your eyes? Do ya need glasses? For the love-a Pete!"

Jack grinned as Dorrie, still fuming and red-faced, plopped back in her seat.

She did a double-take when she saw his smirk. "What're you lookin' at?"

Jack smoothed his expression and adopted his best look of innocence. "Why, not a thing, my little petunia. Why ever would you ask?"

"You better not be lookin' at me like that. Did ya see that play? I coulda made a better throw than that! I *have* made better throws than that!"

He tsked and wagged his finger. "Remember, good Christian manners, dear."

"Oh, park it," she fumed.

The quarterback made a snap, and Jack did his impossible best to shoot to his feet. "I don't believe it!" he bellowed. "He did it again! Hey, you lousy excuse for an athlete! If you were on a ship right now, I'd think you were a double agent for the enemy! If you can't beat the Army, who can you beat?"

"Hey, bud," someone from the row behind said. "Keep your opinions to yourself, why don'tcha?"

Jack couldn't turn around to look, but Dorrie had no such limitations.

"Hey, don't start anything," she warned the man behind. "This isn't a battlefield, it's just a game."

"I'll bet he's wearing Army green," Jack said.

"You got a problem with that?" the protester growled.

"Why, no, sir," Jack politely answered. "I have no problem with the Army at all. Outside of the fact that they'd probably get seasick in a bathtub."

Jack heard just the sound he wanted, a roar like a wounded bear. For a fleeting moment, he wondered if God was taking notes and if his eternal security was in danger. What would Drew have done in this situation? He probably would have bought the guy a hot dog.

In the next instant, a sergeant in an Army uniform came around. He scowled and jerked his head at Jack's chair. "You've got me at a disadvantage, there, Mr. Navy."

Jack popped his chewing gum and gave the man his widest and most enchanting grin. "Frustrating, ain't it?"

Dorrie nudged him. "Jack, don't forget, we're here with the church. Everybody's watchin'!"

The sergeant raised an eyebrow. "What happened? Trip over an anchor?"

"Two squads of Japanese planes and a Bofors forty-millimeter gun."

"Did anybody ever tell you two that you're on the same side?" Dorrie asked, bemused.

"Not today, we're not," Army declared.

"Navy'll beat ya," Jack challenged.

"Army'll bury ya."

"I'll bury ya both!" Dorrie snapped. She pointed at Army. "You, back where ya belong." She turned to Jack. "You! Shut up and watch the game."

Army reluctantly returned to his seat.

Dorrie gave Jack a look of exasperation and held a hand out to the side, palm up. "Did ya even hear the words that just came outta your mouth? Could ya have disrespected our fightin' men any more than ya did?"

"What?" Jack asked, surprised. "I'm not talking about the men in the field. I'm talking about the players. Besides, he had as much fun with it as I did. He's just frustrated that the Army's losing so bad. I did him a favor. He got to blow off steam."

Jack felt a firm hand on his shoulder from behind. Army dug his fingers in.

Jack winced but didn't react. He'd endured worse battle injuries.

Dorrie nudged Jack and jerked her head in Army's direction. "Apologize to the man."

"You know," Jack complained to Dorrie. "You're turning into a regular henpecker."

"I said, apologize."

Jack hesitated, then turned his head as much as possible in Army's direction. "Pal, I didn't hear what I was saying 'til the words got out. Heat of the game. Sorry 'bout what I said about the Army. You guys are doing a great job out there. I know how it goes. I didn't mean any disrespect."

The man took back his hand.

"Of course," Jack muttered under his breath, "You could still learn to play ball a little better."

Dorrie closed her eyes and shook her head.

The next play on the field was better. By the end of the third quarter, Army had no chance of catching up.

When the game ended with Navy victorious, Jack felt happier than he had in years. He was just about to say he'd apologize to the pastor later about his behavior when he heard his name.

"Jackson! Nah, that can't be old meathead Jackson!" A moment later, a face appeared in Jack's field of vision.

Jack's jaw plummeted. "Smitty!"

Smitty leaned over and grasped his hand in a firm handshake. "Jackson, when I heard the noise over here during the end of the third, I knew it hadda be you!" He laughed, then sobered abruptly, really seeing the chair for the first time. "I guess I didn't do a good enough job getting you to the corpsman."

Chapter Forty-One

Jack couldn't stop gawking. After a second, his brain finally kicked back in, but his eyes stayed wide. "Smitty?" he repeated. He shook his head to clear it. "I can't believe—*Smitty*! How can you be here?"

Dorrie stood and moved into a vacant seat. Some kind of reunion was taking place. She didn't want to get in the way. The church group, just about to descend on them, seemed to realize the same thing and turned, deciding to return later.

Without looking at her, Smitty sat in the seat she'd just left.

Jack laughed incredulously and pumped his hand. "Smitty!"

"Whoever woulda thought we'd be here shaking hands like old pals?" Smitty grinned. "The Navy finally got fed up with me. Honorable discharge. How about that? Too many medals for them to just stick me in the brig, I guess. Anyway, whattaya mean what am I doin' here? There isn't a gob in town who isn't here today!"

Curious, Dorrie tapped Jack's elbow. "Ya gonna introduce us?"

Jack started. He'd forgotten where he was. "Hey, Smit, I want to introduce you to my friend Dorrie."

Smitty turned an expectant grin on Dorrie. His expression froze.

Dorrie took his hand. "Glad to meet ya! I guess you're an old Navy buddy of Jack's, huh?"

Smitty shook her hand but looked puzzled. "You're not—" he stammered. "That is, I thought Jackson was gonna marry—"

"Well, he didn't," Dorrie said. "Don't ya listen to the radio or read the papers?"

Smitty shook his head. "Not if I can help it."

"Dorrie is Drew's girl," Jack explained.

Smitty's face lit up. "No foolin'! Hey!" He grabbed her hand again and shook it more enthusiastically. "Brackman's girl! Hey, how about that! Brackman's girl!"

Dorrie stared hard at Jack's friend. There was something about the guy's name. Smitty, Smitty—*Smitty*! "Hey!" She dropped his hand. "You're the guy who gave Jack and Drew such a hard time on the ship!"

He looked uncomfortable.

"Then that also means you're the guy who saved Jack's life."

Smitty nodded. "That's right."

"Well, look at me, meetin' ya like this!" Dorrie grinned. She leaned across Jack and bussed his cheek with a kiss. "It's good to meet ya, Smitty!"

"Likewise!" Smitty beamed. He looked at Jack. "She's all right! The Kid had good taste."

"'Course he did," Dorrie said. "So did I."

Smitty grinned and said, "Listen, I've gotta get back. You in town long?"

"Yeah, here with my church group," Jack said. "Not too far outside Manhattan."

"No foolin'!" Smitty exclaimed. "You got a church group, too?"

Jack stared at him. "Don't tell me you—"

"Saved, baptized, the whole shebang. Navy chaplain got hold of me." He raised his eyebrows. "Just in time, too. I was about ready to take a permanent dip in the Bay." He slapped a hand on Jack's shoulder. "Say, do you have time for a sandwich or somethin' before we call it a day?" He remembered his manners and said to Dorrie, "You, too, ma'am."

She stood. "You two think I want to sit around and listen to ya swap Navy stories?" She smiled to show she was kidding. "I'm gonna have that picnic lunch on the bus with the church. How 'bout I meet ya back here in an hour and a half or so, Jack?"

He nodded.

"There's a place not too far away I can get you to," Smitty said. "They've got a little shack with heaters and food set up for the game. "The guys on the ship oughta see us now, eh, Jackson?"

"They'd never believe it. I just wish *Drew* could see us."

"What? And give the runt the satisfaction?"

Smitty got behind Jack's chair to direct him out of the stands. He gave Dorrie a salute as they left.

***

The makeshift eatery was busy. Although there were no restaurants near West Point, a shed with tables and chairs had been set up.

From the front, Jack and Smitty eyed the crowd. Most of the patrons were young. More than half were servicemen with dates or trying to find dates. The rest were middle-aged locals who'd come to enjoy the game.

The atmosphere was friendly. The sounds of laughter and foolishness drifting around Jack felt like old times. Sometimes, lately, he felt like an old man whose youth was so far behind it was gone forever. This place reminded him he'd only just turned twenty-five. He relaxed and felt glad they'd come.

The logistics weren't great for getting through the shoulder-to-shoulder revelers and around the tightly packed tables.

"This thing has a few disadvantages," Jack said, hitting the arm of the heavy chair.

"Nah," Smitty said. "No different from gettin' through the passageways on the *Bay* or *Yorker*."

A young man in an Army uniform at a table near the front noticed their dilemma. He also realized that these days, seeing a guy as young as Jack in a wheelchair meant one thing. "Hey, man," he said, approaching, beer in hand. "How'd you get the wheels?" The question was without malice.

Jack smirked. "Playin' chicken with the Japanese in the Pacific."

The soldier hooded his eyes. "Navy, huh?"

"Is there anything else?" Smitty asked.

The soldier grinned. "You bet there is! But hey, believe it or not, they tell me we're all on the same side in here now that the game's over." He walked to a table near the door, with several young men in army uniforms seated around it. He kicked the leg of a chair. "Hey, you guys, get up," he demanded.

Jack wasn't sure whether to be grateful or feel embarrassed. "No, thanks," he said. "We'll wait for one to clear."

"Hey, brother, take the table. We were just leavin'," the soldier who'd approached them said.

"What're you talkin' about?" one of his companions complained. "We just got here!"

The soldier kicked his ankle.

"Watch the boot!" the man at the table complained. "Those aren't sneakers you're wearing!"

"Don't listen to this chump," the young man said to Jack and Smitty.

They took the table when it was obvious their new Army ally wouldn't let his friends keep their seats.

"Keep pluggin', Navy," the soldier said, saluting them both. He shook Smitty's hand and thumped Jack's shoulder as he left.

"Hey!" Jack called after him. "You coming or going?"

The young man looked back. "Going. Just got out of boot camp. Gonna have a lot better luck than you did, Navy!"

Jack gave him a thumbs-up. The Kid returned it and was gone.

A cute waitress approached and asked for Jack's and Smitty's orders. Jack ordered a sandwich and a glass of iced tea. Smitty ordered the same.

Although the waitress was young and attractive, she didn't tempt Jack to look twice. There was only one dame on his mind lately.

It was disconcerting to him, though, that the waitress didn't give him a second look, either. He was still the best-looking guy in the room, but the wheelchair made him invisible.

"So, what happened?" Smitty asked.

"What do you mean?"

"What happened to the little movie star? I almost got my face broke over her. I figured you must've liked her a little."

Jack leaned back in the chair. "I cut her loose."

Smitty didn't look convinced. "*You* dumped *her*?

"Yeah, after I realized she wasn't looking forward to taking care of a guy in a wheelchair the rest of her life, I let her go." He shrugged. "I don't have any bad feelings for her."

Smitty grimaced. "That stinks, Jackson."

"Nah. I put myself in her place. Her career is picking up. She worked hard for it. She didn't ask for this. Besides, if she hadn't felt that way, Dorrie and I probably wouldn't be such good friends."

Jack told him how Dorrie had brought him Drew's Navy Cross when he was in the hospital and how she'd been a steady companion during the months of hospitalization and rehabilitation. He told him how Dorrie had led him to the Lord using Drew's ticket analogy.

"Some dames are all class," Smitty vowed. "Brackman's ticket got me thinking, too. I don't think that chaplain would've stood a chance with me if I hadn't heard Brackman talk about that. It got me thinking."

He hesitated. "Y'know. I thought getting back to the States was gonna change things. But somehow, bein' in San Diego made it worse. Too quiet." He shrugged. "When I met you on the *Yorker* that first time, I was already half gone. I saw things on the *Bay* that made what happened on *Yorker* look tame."

Jack nodded. "I knew you were in trouble the first time I saw you."

"Unger knew it, too, but he stuck by me. He knew I was ready to quit before we got to the *Yorker*. Funny how the Navy never figured it out." He tapped Jack's arm. "For what it's worth, Unger liked you. He just couldn't let you know 'cause he was lookin' out for me."

"I know."

"I think about little Tom Peterson sometimes."

"The Kid. Your pal."

Smitty nodded. "Yeah. Boot sailor. Not three months outta ammunition school when the *Bay* got hit. He didn't see the worst of it, but he saw enough. He kinda latched onto me and Unger after that." He raised an eyebrow. "I'd say it was sorta like you and

Brackman, but it wasn't. Brackman was a kid, but he wasn't a *kid*, if you know what I mean."

Jack hadn't thought about it like that, but it was true.

Smitty laughed. "That Dorrie of his is a pistol, I can tell! She's nothin' like Brackman! How'd those two get together?"

Jack snorted. "Probably the same reason Drew and I were pals. Drew was quiet, so he probably got a kick out of being around somebody who didn't care what anybody thought. All I know is that the Lord put both of them in my way for a good reason."

Smitty nodded. "God has a way of findin' us, for sure. When it happened to me, I had to go back and forgive people, whether they were alive or dead. The hardest one was Demy Powell. He was a bad guy. Liked makin' people feel stupid, especially me. 'Cause of him, a lot of guys got killed. A lot."

Jack grimaced. "And you thought I was like him."

"You just look like him, that's all. The way you took care of your little pal—well, I knew you weren't the same as him, but I didn't have any other place to put my mad. You were a good target."

Jack let him talk.

When their food came and the waitress was gone, Jack said, "So, what's next for you, Smit?"

"Got family in Iowa, I think I'll track down."

"You're a landlubber?" Jack said, surprised. "What made you decide to join the Navy all the way out there?"

"Wanted to get as far away as I could from everything I grew up with," Smitty snorted. "Stupid to think I was tryin' to get away from bad, when bad's all I ran into when I got into the Navy." He jerked his head at Jack. "What about you?"

Jack hesitated before answering. "I don't know. I was thinking about becoming a choreographer."

Smitty looked confused.

"Write out steps for dancers," Jack said.

"Oh," Smitty said with a nod.

"Besides that, maybe I'll get married." Jack's own words startled him.

Smitty didn't seem surprised. "Brackman's girl?" he asked.

Jack smiled. "My girl."

Chapter Forty-Two

Getting Jack home was no simple task. The wheelchair weighed fifty pounds and took two men to lift into the back of the church bus. They'd adapted the vehicle for the chair before his release from rehabilitation by removing three rows of seats at the back.

Jack felt humiliated that he had to be lifted and settled into a seat by men from the church, too old to be involved in the war. He swallowed his pride, but the sting persisted.

He gazed out the window as the bus pulled away from the West Point grounds.

Less than a year earlier, he'd expertly handled high-powered military guns. A few years before that, his name had been in lights on Broadway. Now here he was, twenty-five years old, and he felt the Lord had already written the best years of his life.

They tell me you know best, Lord, he prayed inwardly. *I have to trust that you do.*

Dorrie sat beside him on the ride back to Mount Vernon from West Point.

"How'd your lunch go with Smitty?" she asked.

"Good," he said. "There was a lot to talk about. He's got plenty to work through."

"And you don't?" Dorrie asked.

He considered that. “I have flashes,” he admitted. “Dreams sometimes, but I’ve been able to keep ‘em from eating me alive. Some guys never get there.” He thought of big, blustering Smitty, who’d intimidated him and Drew the first time they’d seen him board the ramp to the *Yorker*. “Sometimes, the louder they are, the more they have to hide.”

Dorrie laced her arm through his. “Those guys out there are just people,” she mused. “On both sides.”

He shot her a startled look.

“Don’t look at me like that,” she admonished. “I’m not defendin’ what the Japanese or the Germans are doin’. All I have to do is think about Drew or look at ya to hold a giant-size grudge against ‘em. Besides, I’d like to keep America the way it is, thank ya very much.

“But Jesus died for everybody, and I hate to think of anybody windin’ up in hell, especially gettin’ there after bein’ in a battle.” She raised her eyebrows. “Outta the fryin’ pan.” She shook her head. “Nah, I don’t wish that on anybody.”

He tried to understand her point of view and even saw where she was coming from, but the memory of men he’d known lying dead at his feet after some battles kept him from it.

“You had to be there,” he said.

She nodded. “I know. Easy for me to talk.” She laid her head against his shoulder.

When they arrived at the church, the bus pulled up as close as possible to Jack’s little one-bedroom cottage on the grounds. They pulled the heavy wheelchair out of the back.

Once on the pavement, Jack’s helpers settled him into the seat.

“Need any help inside, Jack?” the pastor asked.

“I’ll help if he needs it,” Dorrie said. She gave Jack a questioning look.

He nodded. “Yeah, come on in.”

The pastor nodded and headed back.

“Bye, Jack!” friends from the bus waved as the vehicle pulled out.

“Thanks for the lift, sailors!” Dorrie giggled.

Jack grinned. “Where’d you come from, you dippy dame?”

She took offense at the lesser insult. “Who’re you callin’ a dame?” She got behind the chair to push him toward the door.

“I’ve got it,” he said. At the door, he removed his key and inserted it into the lock.

The apartment was little more than a large cube with a bedroom and bathroom near the back. During his time in rehabilitation, the church had worked hard to adapt doorways, windows, and fixtures. They’d even rebuilt counters and cabinets to make it easier for him to live a normal life.

There was little furniture, but they’d provided a table with wide legs, two chairs, and a bed. Women from the church had sewn a quilt for the bed. Dorrie provided window coverings and helped him clean the area once or twice a week.

“Y’know,” she mused when they were inside. “They’ve made this place so great for ya. I know ya want to pick out your own house someday, but it’ll never be as good as this.”

He nodded. “Yeah, it’s perfect. Almost makes me feel normal.” He shrugged. “I’ll cross that bridge when I come to it. You want tea?”

“Sure. I’ll get it.”

“No, I can do it. Sit down.”

She obliged and watched as he put the kettle on the stove and took cups and tea bags from the lower shelves. “Nobody’d know ya were in the hospital for so long,” she mused. “You’re doin’ great, Jack. I’m proud-a ya.”

“Couldn’t have done it without you,” he said. “I feel like I dodged a bullet. I could have married Loretta.”

She frowned. “Hey, bud, that’s not fair. Loretta’s a good girl. I betcha she just couldn’t handle what happened.”

“Yeah. Give me a hand here. I can’t move the chair and handle the cups at the same time.”

She jumped up. “Oh, sure.”

When they settled at the table, he said. “I don’t hold anything against Loretta. She should never have been out there. The Navy shouldn’t have let any of that happen.”

“How’d you live with that kind of stuff every day?” she asked. “You’re only human.”

"Conditioned to it," he said, then snorted. "Nah, that's not true. You do what you have to do, or you curl up in a ball and die. But at least I was trained for it. Loretta was there to give a show. I don't blame her for backing out."

"What did ya mean about dodgin' a bullet 'cause you mighta married her?"

No woman had ever made him feel nervous, but now he wondered if he could get his words out. "'Cause if I'd married her, I couldn't ask *you* to marry me."

It didn't click for her at first. She nodded, then her eyes widened. "What did you just say?"

"You deaf?"

"Maybe so. I thought I just heard ya say somethin' about marriage."

"Nothing wrong with your ears."

He waited expectantly.

She hesitated, then her mouth turned up at one end in a coy smile. "What makes you think I'd want to marry you?"

"Well," he mugged, "outside of my charm, good looks, and amazing personality, I can't think of a thing."

She snorted. "You'll have to do better than that."

He thought a moment, then looked up, inspired. "How about I'm the only guy you know who has his very own wheelchair?"

She giggled, then burst into laughter. "That'll do it!" She came around to his side of the table. "I'll marry ya, and I'll tell ya why. Nobody else is crazy enough to do it." She kissed him sweetly.

He deepened the kiss.

She pulled back with a look of surprise. "Gee whiz!"

He grinned and put his hands on either side of her face. "I have a feeling that my life is about to get really strange."

THE END

www.ingramcontent.com/pod-product-compliance
Lightning Source LLC
LaVergne TN
LVHW090603110826
845146LV00001B/241

9798999928016